# AVAILABLE NOW!

### LEARNING TO RIDE

City girl Madeline Harper never wanted to love a cowboy. But rodeo king Tanner Callen might change her mind...and win her heart.

### THE McCULLAGH INN IN MAINE

Chelsea O'Kane escapes to Maine to build a new life—until she runs into Jeremy Holland, an old flame....

### SACKING THE QUARTERBACK

Attorney Melissa St. James wins every case. Now, when she's up against football superstar Grayson Knight, her heart is on the line, too.

### THE MATING SEASON

Documentary ornithologist Sophie Castle is convinced that her heart belongs only to the birds—until she meets her gorgeous cameraman, Rigg Greensman.

### THE RETURN

Ashley Montoya was in love with Mack McLeroy in high school—until he broke her heart. But when an accident brings him back home to Sunnybell to recover, Ashley can't help but fall into his embrace....

### DAZZLING: THE DIAMOND TRILOGY, BOOK I

To support her artistic career, Siobhan Dempsey works at the elite Stone Room in New York City…never expecting to be swept away by Derick Miller.

### BODYGUARD

Special Agent Abbie Whitmore has only one task: protect Congressman Jonathan Lassiter from a violent cartel's threats. Yet she's never had to do it while falling in love.…

# BOOK**SHOTS**

### CROSS KILL

*Along Came a Spider* killer Gary Soneji died years ago. But Alex Cross swears he sees Soneji gun down his partner. Is his greatest enemy back from the grave?

### ZOO 2

Humans are evolving into a savage new species that could save civilization—or end it. James Patterson's *Zoo* was just the beginning.

### THE TRIAL

An accused killer will do anything to disrupt his own trial, including a courtroom shocker that Lindsay Boxer and the Women's Murder Club will never see coming.

### LITTLE BLACK DRESS

Can a little black dress change everything? What begins as one woman's fantasy is about to go too far.

### LET'S PLAY MAKE-BELIEVE

Christy and Marty just met, and it's love at first sight. Or is it? One of them is playing a dangerous game—and only one will survive.

### CHASE

A man falls to his death in an apparent accident....But why does he have the fingerprints of another man who is already dead? Detective Michael Bennett is on the case.

### HUNTED

Someone is luring men from the streets to play a mysterious, high-stakes game. Former Special Forces officer David Shelley goes undercover to shut it down—but will he win?

### 113 MINUTES

Molly Rourke's son has been murdered. Now she'll do whatever it takes to get justice. No one should underestimate a mother's love....

### $10,000,000 MARRIAGE PROPOSAL

A mysterious billboard offering $10 million to get married intrigues three single women in LA. But who is Mr. Right...and is he the perfect match for the lucky winner?

### FRENCH KISS

It's hard enough to move to a new city, but now everyone French detective Luc Moncrief cares about is being killed off. Welcome to New York.

### KILLER CHEF

Caleb Rooney knows how to do two things: run a food truck and solve a murder. When people suddenly start dying of food-borne illnesses, the stakes are higher than ever....

## UPCOMING ROMANCES

### RADIANT: THE DIAMOND TRILOGY, BOOK II

After an explosive breakup with her billionaire boyfriend, Siobhan Dempsey moves to Detroit to pursue her art. But Derick isn't ready to give her up.

### HOT WINTER NIGHTS

Allie Thatcher moved to Montana to start fresh as the head of the trauma center. And even though the days are cold, the nights are steamy...especially when she meets search-and-rescue leader Dex Belmont.

## UPCOMING THRILLERS
### BOOK**SHOTS**

### THE CHRISTMAS MYSTERY

Two stolen paintings disappear from a Park Avenue murder scene—
French detective Luc Moncrief is in for a merry Christmas.

### COME AND GET US

When an SUV deliberately runs Miranda Cooper and her husband
off a desolate Arizona road, she must run for help alone as his cryp-
tic parting words echo in her head: "Be careful who you trust."

### BLACK & BLUE

Detective Harry Blue is determined to take down the serial killer
who's abducted several women, but her mission leads to a shocking
revelation.

## A PERFECT MATCH

Siobhan came to New York with a purpose: she wants to become a successful artist. To pay her bills in the meantime, she's the hostess at the Stone Room, a bar for the beautiful and the billionaires. She's fine with being on her own—until tech billionaire Derick takes her breath away.

**Read the first book in the Diamond Trilogy, *Dazzling*, available now from**

# Bodyguard

## An Under Covers Story

## JESSICA LINDEN

FOREWORD BY

## JAMES PATTERSON

*James Patterson's*
BOOK**SHOTS** *Flames*

BookShots

Little, Brown and Company

New York Boston London

BookShots / Little, Brown and Company
Hachette Book Group
1290 Avenue of the Americas, New York, NY 10104
bookshots.com

First Edition: November 2016

BookShots is an imprint of Little, Brown and Company, a division of Hachette Book Group, Inc. The Little, Brown name and logo are trademarks of Hachette Book Group, Inc. The BookShots name and logo are trademarks of JBP Business, LLC.

The publisher is not responsible for websites (or their content) that are not owned by the publisher.

The Hachette Speakers Bureau provides a wide range of authors for speaking events. To find out more, go to hachettespeakersbureau.com or call (866) 376-6591.

ISBN 978-0-316-32014-6
LCCN 2016938305

10 9 8 7 6 5 4 3 2 1

LSC-C

Printed in the United States of America

# FOREWORD

When I first had the idea for BookShots, I knew that I wanted to include romantic stories. The whole point of BookShots is to give people lightning-fast reads that completely capture them for just a couple of hours in their day—so publishing romance felt right.

I have a lot of respect for romance authors. I took a stab at the genre when I wrote *Suzanne's Diary for Nicholas* and *Sundays at Tiffany's*. While I was happy with the results, I learned that the process of writing those stories required hard work and dedication.

That's why I wanted to pair up with the best romance authors for BookShots. I work with writers who know how to draw emotions out of their characters, all while catapulting their plots forward.

Because you have this book in your hands, you're about to be engrossed by Jonathan and Abbie's story in *Bodyguard*. Since Abbie heads up the security detail on Jonathan's campaign tour, they're in a situation that makes it unlikely for the two of them to fall in love. Yet author Jessica Linden writes chemistry that is absolutely magnetic, all while she flips romantic tropes on their heads. You'll be blown away.

James Patterson

# Bodyguard

## An Under Covers Story

# Chapter 1

ABBIE WHITMORE STOOD at the back of the crowd at the steps of the town hall, easily blending in with the mass of people also dressed in somber dark suits. She wasn't scheduled to arrive until later that evening, but she preferred doing recon in person, instead of just reading a case file.

This was an eye-opening experience. Though she lived outside of DC, she didn't pay attention to politics. It was all a sham. Though politicians had some margin of power, she knew there were other players who pulled the strings in Washington.

She zoned in on the charismatic man on the podium. The pairing of his suit and tie was impeccable, and no doubt the work of a professional. His dark hair was styled in such a way that it didn't look like anything had been done to it at all. It matched well with his five-o'clock shadow.

Men and women of all ages cheered after nearly every sentence he spoke, pressing forward to try to get closer to him, as if proximity would cause some of his charm and charisma to rub off on them.

The Beloved Bachelor of Capitol Hill…that was what the society pages had called him—a completely cumbersome title, but if the shoe fit…However, his bachelor status wasn't why she was here. She was here because he was too golden for his own good.

And someone was going to kill him for it.

"Just remember"—he stopped to flash a blindingly brilliant smile—"I hear you and I am here for you."

The crowd erupted, shaking signs, hooting, and hollering. If she didn't know better, Abbie would think she was at a Justin Bieber concert.

Lord help her.

Jonathan Lassiter gave one last wave, then exited the stage using the rickety wooden stairs that had been erected on the left.

That was her cue.

She ducked her head down and strode through the throngs of people, heading in the direction of the parked car waiting to whisk the politician away. Even though she flanked his team, swinging wide to avoid detection, she still beat him there. He was too busy posing for selfies.

*Wonder if he'll have to sign anyone's breasts.* Abbie almost snorted.

Once at the far side of the car, she reached into her purse to pull out a thin metal wire. On a whim she tried the door handle first, shaking her head when it was unlocked.

*Amateurs. It's a wonder he hasn't been killed already.*

She slid into the backseat of the car, and no one was the wiser.

She didn't have to wait long.

The driver opened the door, and with one final wave Jonathan Lassiter took his seat across from her.

In one swift move Abbie extended her leg and lodged the base of her shoe on his Adam's apple, the toe and the heel of the shoe straddling his neck. Game over.

"If I wanted you dead, you would be."

Jonathan blinked, and swallowed with some difficulty. Though she had to hand it to him—he kept his cool. "Do you mind removing your Louboutin from my jugular?"

Abbie's response was to apply more pressure and narrow her eyes at him.

Then, slowly, she lowered her leg.

# Chapter 2

"YOU MIGHT NOT want to be so blasé about your safety."

Jonathan adjusted his tie and studied the woman sitting across from him. At first glance, she appeared sweet and vulnerable, like she was one of those women who followed the trend of too-thin supermodels. His instincts also told him that there was more to her than her looks.

He'd felt the muscles in her long leg firsthand when her red-soled stiletto was rammed under his chin. *Frail* was not the word for her.

Lithe. That's what she was. This wasn't a woman who dieted to keep her trim figure.

Her copper hair was pulled tight at the nape of her neck, making her cheekbones appear even more severe and angular. The creamy skin on her face showed no signs of freckles, and her makeup was barely there. She was a natural beauty.

And her eyes were so goddamn cold and calculating she'd rival any supermodel on the runway. He would know. He'd dated a few of them.

The car pulled away from the sidewalk, his driver unaware that anything unusual was happening in the backseat.

Jonathan adjusted his cuff links. "You weren't due to arrive until this evening."

"Change of plans."

"If you had done me the courtesy of contacting my people, I could have arranged to set up a proper first meeting." He smiled at her. "You wouldn't have had to break into my car."

"I didn't," she said smartly. "It was unlocked. You take your safety seriously for granted, Mr. Lassiter."

"I'm a man of the people," he replied. "I like to be available to my constituents. After all, they're the reason I'm here."

"Perhaps they'll enjoy attending your funeral as well."

He chuckled. "I doubt that."

She reached into her bag, pulled out a thick file folder, and slapped it on his lap. "Copies of phone transcriptions and intercepted e-mails. All threats against you."

He leafed through the papers, but they weren't anything he hadn't seen before. His team back in the capital had showed him similar documents last week, before he'd set out on the campaign trail. It had taken a call from the White House for him to accept personal security above and beyond what he felt was reasonable and needed.

The woman sitting across from him was the last thing he'd expected.

"I meant I doubt these threats will amount to anything."

"Regardless, they shouldn't be ignored."

Jonathan closed the file and handed it back to her. "You never introduced yourself, Miss…?"

"Abbie Whitmore." She didn't bother to hold out her hand but instead scrutinized him with her cold eyes.

"Miss Whitmore, I'm afraid your presence here is an overreaction on the part of my well-meaning associates. If special protection were assigned to politicians every time a threat was made against them, well…" He trailed off and chuckled. Then he unbuttoned his suit coat, making himself comfortable.

Her nostrils flared slightly. "You may not take the threats against your life seriously, but I take my job very seriously. So I plan to have the pleasure of keeping you alive for the foreseeable future."

He met her hard stare with one of his own, one that made lesser individuals stand down. She held her ground.

"Fine," he said tightly. He knew when to cut his losses. Besides, it wouldn't be much of a hardship to have this gorgeous woman following him around for the next few weeks.

"The plan is to introduce me to your staff as a new aide who you'll be working very closely with. I don't want them to know my real purpose for being here."

He frowned. "Isn't that a bit extreme?"

"No. What's extreme is what might be done if Hak Tanir gets to you. The last guy who crossed them was disemboweled, before taking two slugs between the eyes at point-blank range. His own mother couldn't recognize what was left of him."

She flashed a picture on her cell phone to reiterate her point. The blood drained from his face, and much to his disconcertment, she gave a little nod of satisfaction, putting her phone away.

"The legislation you spearheaded allowed the US government to make large strides in stopping Hak Tanir and several of the human-trafficking rings they're responsible for. As a result, you now have some dangerous enemies in some pretty high places."

"I wasn't the only one who supported that bill."

"No, but you were, and are, the spokesman for it."

He shifted. "They can't possibly think that killing me will stop us from trying to put an end to terrorism."

"I doubt they think that. What's done is done. But now they're out for vengeance. Or perhaps they want to make an example out of you. Either way, you're in need of protection beyond the normal detail assigned to a congressman on the campaign trail."

"I will gladly let you join my team, but this can't interrupt my reelection efforts," he said firmly, the blood having returned to his face. "That legislation was just the beginning. There's still a lot more work to be done."

The disdain that had lined the edges of her face shifted slightly, morphing into something else. She nodded again, only this time he thought he detected a hint of respect.

"You aren't any help to anyone if you're dead."

# Chapter 3

JONATHAN STARED AT Abbie incredulously, like the words she was saying didn't make sense.

"How else can I shake their hands?" His tone was exasperated, and he'd been pulling at his hair so much that it was standing on end.

And damn if that didn't make him sexier. It only made her dislike him more.

Abbie crossed her arms. "That's my whole point. No one should be allowed to come close enough to touch you."

"I'm not the goddamn queen of England." He loosened the tie at his neck and undid the top two buttons of his shirt, then collapsed into the chair.

Abbie's eyebrows rose. The security measures she wanted to implement weren't even that severe, but the usually smooth politician was becoming unglued.

*Good,* she decided. He *shouldn't* be comfortable. Someone wanted to kill him. She'd thought she made the situation clear to him in the limo yesterday, but he was still fighting her.

He sighed. "My platform is built on being a man for the people. It's what I'm known for. But it's more than that. That's who I want to be. That's why I got into public service. I'm not some elitist who isolates himself from the people he represents."

Before she could stop it, a bitter laugh escaped her lips. "You are the definition of an elitist. You grew up in one of the wealthiest families in America."

*Shit.* She'd just crossed a line. She didn't have to like the guy—or where he came from—to keep him alive.

It had taken her two days to place him. Besides seeing him on the news, she could have sworn she knew him from somewhere, but nothing in his file indicated that they would have crossed paths.

But she'd figured it out this morning. He had been friends with her ex, the asshole she'd dated all through college. The man she had thought she'd marry. And the man she apparently hadn't been good enough for.

He'd blindsided her when he ditched her for a socialite who could further his law career. So she'd accepted a position with the Cartwright Agency and never looked back.

At first she'd been concerned that Jonathan would have remembered her, too. But after remembering him in that limo, she knew it was an unfounded worry.

She might as well be just another woman seeking to take a selfie with him. He didn't have a clue who she was.

And she felt stupid for thinking he might.

Jonathan's face hardened at her words, making him seem dangerous. Abbie was impressed, and her respect for him went up a notch. She hadn't thought this pretty-boy politician had it in him. She waited for his response. "I don't see how my upbringing is relevant to your current assignment. But for the sake of being cooperative, is there anything else about my life you'd like to discuss before we move on?"

"You're a politician," she said, dismissing his question. "Your life is public record."

The truth was she had everything in his file, right down to his shoe size. She was nothing if not prepared.

"That's not what I asked."

Abbie sat at the table and rubbed her temples. At twenty-nine, she was one of the youngest agents at Cartwright to have taken on solo assignments. She'd protected witnesses from the Mob while they were waiting to testify at trial, before sending them on their way in the Witness Security Program. She'd gone undercover in a gang in Chicago to protect a confidential informant. She'd even spent time in LA guarding an A-list actress from a stalker.

And none of them had proven to be as difficult as Congressman Jonathan Lassiter.

Because all of them had *wanted* protection. They understood the danger they were in.

Jonathan didn't seem to get that. Trying to get that through to him was like beating her head against a brick wall.

And all she really wanted to do was pound *his* head against a brick wall.

"Do you have any family members or close friends who may be targeted?" Abbie asked, looking up from her file.

Jonathan drummed his fingers on the tabletop. "No."

Abbie sighed and pulled off her reading glasses. "No one? Are you sure? No close friends? Ex-girlfriends? Girl-friends?"

He narrowed his piercing blue eyes at her, and she felt it.

She quickly looked away. She'd stared down murderers and rapists without flinching, but those sexy blue eyes were too much. Too intense.

*Pull it together, Whitmore.*

"Doesn't your file tell you everything about me?"

"Almost, but I like to be thorough. Besides, you may have developed a relationship since this information was compiled." It wasn't likely, but she had to check.

He stared at her a beat longer than necessary before answering. "No, there's no one."

She felt a faint heat rising to her cheeks, and she cleared her throat and hastily shoved her glasses back onto her face.

What the hell was that about? She *never* blushed. Wait… was she *attracted* to him? That wasn't happening. She would *not* get the hots for her assignment. That was against the cardinal rule of being a bodyguard.

But the way Jonathan looked at her…she was starting to understand why some overzealous women had set up a Facebook fan club for him, posting shirtless paparazzi pictures from his recent beach vacation.

"That's good," she said. When his eyebrows shot up, she couldn't fight off the blush this time. She ignored it and forged ahead. "Because then there's no one else at risk."

He nodded, saying nothing, and continued to stare at her. She wasn't fooled by his silence, though. He wasn't giving in to her.

She folded her hands on the table. "What? Lay it out there."

"I'll do everything you want me to do as long as it doesn't interfere with my campaign."

She ripped off her glasses again. If she spent too much more time with Jonathan, the damn things were going to end up broken.

"How's that going to work? How can I protect you if you won't follow my instructions?"

"Meeting the constituents is important to me." Although his tone was calm and controlled, the muscle in his jaw worked, giving away his frustration.

Why didn't this man get it? His *life* was in danger, and he was worried about shaking hands with every damn person he came in contact with?

*He cares more about them than himself.* She suddenly got it. She'd thought his "man of the people" routine was just that— a song and dance to win votes. But here she was, face-to-face with a politician who genuinely cared.

*They do exist.* Just her luck to get stuck with the one honest politician.

Begrudgingly, she had to admit that his dedication was admirable.

She took a deep breath and tried to soften her stern expression. Her friends at the agency called it her RBF, or resting bitch face. She looked young and could easily pass for ten years below her actual age, which had been both a blessing and a curse in her early years on the job. So she'd toughened up her look, and it stuck. Now it was just her normal expression.

"I will try my best," she said slowly, "but my priority is your safety."

"Your best is all I can ask for."

*Spoken like a damn politician.*

# Chapter 4

JONATHAN RAPPED ON Abbie's door first thing the next morning. She'd taken the room next to his, not wanting to be far away. It had been a restless night knowing she was just on the other side of the wall.

He heard a rustling and knew she was looking through the peephole first. He suppressed a smile. Of course she wouldn't be much good at protecting him if she didn't take basic safety precautions for herself.

Maybe she was right. Maybe he did take his safety for granted. But he simply hadn't needed to worry about certain dangers when he was growing up.

Helping dismantle Hak Tanir was his crowning accomplishment. Sure, it looked nice on his resume, but more importantly, stopping them had put an end to a great deal of human trafficking in the US.

That was a horror he could barely wrap his head around.

Abbie opened the door wearing nothing but her skirt and

a silky little top with skinny straps, the kind that women wore under suits.

Without the armor of her suit and with her hair tangled around her shoulders, Abbie looked less like the security specialist badass and more soft—feminine.

*Sexy.*

Oh, she'd been sexy before, but in a more leather-clad-dominatrix way—the type of woman who'd kick a man's ass—and he'd liked it, but this he liked even more.

Now she looked like the type of woman who'd enjoy long walks on the beach, making out, and watching the sunset. The type of woman who made a guy want to make sappy romantic gestures simply for the opportunity to see her smile or, better yet, hold her close.

It didn't escape his notice that she'd been hiding a pair of fantastic breasts under that jacket.

He closed his eyes and rubbed them with his fingers.

Abbie put a hand on his arm. "Are you okay?"

*Fine. Just checking out my bodyguard.*

*Christ.* She wasn't his bodyguard. She was…well, providing extra security, that's all.

"Fine. It's time for the staff meeting."

She frowned and looked at her watch. "I thought I had another twenty minutes."

"You do." He smiled, keeping his eyes carefully trained on her face, lest they wander to inappropriate places. "I thought I'd be a gentleman and walk you to the conference room."

"Oh." She looked taken aback, like it hadn't occurred to her that he might treat her like a lady. "Come in. I'll just be a minute." She disappeared into the bathroom.

He stepped into the room and closed the door behind him, hovering just inside. That didn't hide his view of the room, though.

And the cache of weapons she had laid out on the bed.

He whistled softly and walked over to investigate.

There were four guns, all of varying sizes. He recognized a Glock. Another was a tiny silver thing that he imagined could fit in a small handbag. The other two were black, and that was all he could say about them.

He preferred to do his fighting on the floor of the Capitol Building. Weapons weren't his thing.

Next to the guns were five knives, all of varying lengths and widths. A sheath lay next to each of them. An abandoned sharpening stone sat on the nightstand.

Handcuffs and a spool of wire rounded out the collection.

He didn't even want to know what the wire was for.

The spread made him realize that he was dealing with a highly trained, deadly individual, something that was easy to forget when you were looking at her gorgeous face.

Which he supposed was kind of the point.

She emerged from the bathroom with her hair tied securely at her neck and her crisp blazer in place. She picked up a case beside the bed and laid it open, then proceeded to stow each of the weapons carefully in its proper place, save for the Glock and the small silver gun. She locked the case with a tiny key dangling from a bracelet on her wrist and stored it in the hotel room safe, found in the closet and conveniently bolted to the floor.

"That's some serious hardware," Jonathan commented.

"Tools of the trade." Her tone was matter-of-fact. You'd think she'd just packed away some manicure tools rather than an arsenal of deadly instruments.

She strapped the Glock to her hip, under her blazer. Then she hiked up her skirt and slipped the gun into a holster strapped high up on her shapely thigh.

*Jesus fucking Christ.*

Maybe he'd been right about that dominatrix thing after all. He hadn't thought that was his thing, but for her it could be.

How in the heck did a beautiful young woman get into this line of work? He discerned her to be in her mid to late twenties—he knew better than to ask directly—and judging from the way she handled those weapons, not to mention the way she'd handled him in the limo yesterday, she had a decent amount of experience.

It should make him feel good that he was in such capable hands; instead, it made him curious.

And it made him want to be in her hands *literally* instead of just figuratively.

"Do you like your job?" he asked.

She blinked. "Yes. Why do you ask?"

He crossed his arms and leaned against the wall. "I don't know. It's…I don't want to say an *odd* choice of profession for a woman, because that would make me sexist, but it's definitely a *rare* one."

"Don't worry. I'm good at it."

"I wasn't. That's not why I asked."

She looked skyward and blew out a breath. "Okay, I suppose it's fair to wonder a little about me, especially in light of the fact that I know so much about you. I graduated from Georgetown University with top honors. I also played soccer and had a background in martial arts, so the agency recruited me after graduation. It was the best offer I received, so I took it."

He stared at her, saying nothing. She'd somehow managed to tell him everything and nothing all at once.

"Do you like *your* job?" she asked, changing the subject quickly.

"Of course." He smiled and gestured to her door. "Shall we?"

She nodded. He opened the door for her, and as he walked through, his gaze traveled down the length of her, settling for a few extra seconds on her ass.

It was a fine ass. This woman was definitely in shape—there wasn't an ounce of fat on her, and every muscle was toned.

She glanced over her shoulder with one arched brow, as if she knew where his eyes had been. She probably did. Women had a sixth sense about those things.

So he pasted an innocent expression on his face. He put his hand on the small of her back to guide her to the conference room. He felt her back go rigid, though she didn't slow her pace or look at him.

Interesting. Perhaps he wasn't the only one feeling the spark in the air. But he'd bet his life that he was the only one who would acknowledge it.

# Chapter 5

THE NEXT MORNING, Abbie stormed down the hall and flung open the door to the conference room. She stood in the doorway and seethed for a moment, narrowing her eyes at Jonathan.

He merely raised his eyebrows at her from his position of authority at the head of the table. Staff members lined its sides, their heads swiveling back and forth between Abbie and Jonathan.

Heads would do more than swivel by the time she was done—some were gonna roll.

She stepped into the room and crossed her arms, her feet spread wide in an aggressive stance. "Why was I not informed about the venue change for this morning's rally?"

"Ah, yes." Eugene or Edgar or whatever his name was—something ridiculous, considering he looked barely old enough to shave—pushed his glasses up higher on his nose and noisily flipped through some papers in front of him. "The change was made late last night when we learned the parking garage near the high school was under construction. The elementary school was the best available alternative."

Abbie's steely gaze shifted to him, and he squirmed under her scrutiny. "Thank you for the information, Eugene."

"Uh, it's Earl, actually." He cleared his throat. "My name is Earl."

"Well, *Earl,* changing the venue at the last minute is unacceptable."

"Excuse us, everyone," Jonathan said, flashing his own team his trademark campaign smile. "Do you mind excusing my aide and me for a few moments?"

Earl shot out the door, and the others scurried after him, looking at their toes or the pictures on the wall, basically anything to avoid Abbie's glare.

As they should. They had the sense to fear her, even though they didn't know her true identity. Jonathan, on the other hand, who truly had something to fear, considering the threats on his life, acted like every day was a day at the beach.

There had been no incidents since Abbie had been with him, and she aimed to keep it that way. But every moment that passed when Jonathan was not in active danger made him more and more assured in his opinion that extra security was overkill, especially since the e-mail and telephone threats had ceased.

Jonathan stood and buttoned his suit coat, waiting until the last staff member had left the room and closed the door.

"Might I remind you, Miss Whitmore, that you are here

posing as my aide. Perhaps your cover would be more believable if you acted like one."

In retrospect, going undercover as his aide was probably not the best plan. Normally, she didn't mind fading into the background while on the job, but this man was infuriating and undermining all she was trying to do. Not to mention everything about him pushed her buttons, from his debonair persona to the sexy stubble that peppered his jawline.

"The change of venue presented numerous security threats that I was unable to counter on such short notice. I—"

"I don't think you understand." Jonathan walked around the table to stand across from her, and she had to force herself not to step back. His nearness was intoxicating, but she wouldn't give him the power of knowing how he affected her. "Anyone else who pulled that stunt in the middle of a staff meeting would be fired on the spot."

Abbie's nostrils flared slightly. "Then I guess it's a good thing I'm not your employee."

"Not directly, but you do work for—"

"*No.* Not *for* you. *With* you. I work with you. Or at least I'm trying to. Don't you ever try pulling that superior bullshit." Anger was good. She could deal with anger much better than the other feeling gathering deep inside her belly. "My job here is to keep you alive, and that is more important than anything you have on your political agenda."

He closed the distance between them, standing toe-to-toe with her. "My *agenda,* as you call it, is to continue to represent these people and promote legislation that keeps them safe."

She knew he was trying to intimidate her, but in her heels she was nearly as tall as he was. Besides, she'd faced down scarier men than him and kicked their asses. A playboy politician was no match for her.

Even though he didn't intimidate her, she wasn't immune to his presence. It lit a fire in her, and it wasn't the slow-burning kind—more like an all-consuming destructive heat. The fact that he made her feel this way only fueled her rage.

"You can't legislate if you're dead," she snarled. "Get that through your head."

She turned on her heel to leave, but she took only one step before he grabbed her wrist, yanking her against him.

His eyes, filled with the heat and hunger of a man who'd spent one too many nights alone on the campaign trail, roamed over her face. This was a man who wasn't used to being told what to do.

She should pull away and put him in his place, but he was like a flame and she a moth. The raw masculinity oozing out of him was magnetic.

He crushed his lips to hers, and for a moment she was paralyzed, not sure if she wanted to give in to the need that was eating away at her or slap him across the face.

When his arm encircled her and his hands slid down to cup her ass, she leaned into him. He took it as a sign and deepened the kiss.

*I need to get this out of my system* was her last coherent thought.

Jonathan spun her around, so that her back was to the conference table, and guided her a few steps until the edge of the table touched the backs of her thighs.

God, she made him so fucking hard. Having her lithe body pressed against his drove him to near insanity. But it was more than just that—it was the way she reacted to him. That purring sound in the back of her throat. Her hands tangling in his hair. The sensual look in her eyes.

Something had flipped a switch inside her, turning off the cold, calculating agent and creating a steamy siren. And he was more than happy to take this ride with her.

He gripped her ass tighter and lifted her onto the tabletop. She spread her legs, and he stood between them.

Warmth radiated from her core, and his cock strained against his pants. He ground it against her, harder when she responded to the motion.

His tongue battled with hers. She undid the buttons on his jacket and roughly pushed it down his arms. She ran her fingers over the front of him, and he let her explore all she wanted.

She worked at undoing his shirt buttons before she gave up and simply pulled the shirt apart. Buttons flew, landing on the floor and the table, bouncing with a *tap-tap-tap*.

He tore his mouth away from hers and sucked at her

throat, snaking his hand under her blouse to take her breast in his hand. Her nipple responded immediately to his touch, tightening.

She closed her eyes and tilted her head back, a moan escaping her lips.

It took all his restraint not to rip her clothes off and take her right there on the damn table.

"Fuck." With that one little word she shattered the ambience. She put her palms flat against his chest and pushed him away. Though she stared at him with her eyes raw and full of need, there was a definite chill in the air.

And while she panted, the chill extended to her eyes, and they were once again cold.

She clutched at her jacket, covering her taut nipples, which were poking through her sheer blouse.

Jonathan didn't move, not wanting to take that step back, hoping they could somehow pick up where they'd left off.

But logically he knew that was wishful thinking.

"You can't…I can't…I mean, we can't…" She'd never been so inarticulate. Abbie always knew what to say. This, if nothing else, was proof that he'd gotten to her.

"I'm pretty sure we just were," he said, finally moving away.

She was still sitting on the table with her skirt hiked up and her legs spread, her silk panties just barely concealing her femininity. She hopped down and adjusted her skirt, somehow managing to appear dignified.

"I'm serious about giving me proper notice if there are

changes to your itinerary, no matter how small." Her tone was formal and crisp. You'd never know they'd been minutes away from screwing on the conference table.

She was a damn robot. How the hell could she turn it off so quickly, when his body was still reeling?

He took another step back. "Sure. I'll let my staff know."

"Thank you."

Then she strode out of the room, in much the same manner as she'd entered. There had to be a metaphor in there somewhere.

He stared after her for a moment before he tried to salvage his ruined shirt.

## Chapter 6

ABBIE ROOTED AROUND in her suitcase looking for the perfect blouse. Not because she wanted to impress Jonathan. Quite the opposite. In fact, she wished it were winter so a turtleneck would be acceptable.

She frowned at the once pristinely folded clothing, now crumpled. *Screw this.* She grabbed the first blouse her hand came in contact with and shut the lid of her suitcase. She wasn't going to alter her routine. It wasn't her wardrobe that was the problem, anyway.

It was Jonathan. Or to be more precise, her attraction to him. Even now the memory of his hands on her skin and his mouth on hers lit a fire in her belly and put a flush on her cheeks.

But that didn't change the fact that getting involved with an assignment—especially with a man like him—was unacceptable.

She slid into her blouse, then pulled her jacket over it.

Looking in the mirror, she pulled her hair back into a severe bun, one that said business. And hopefully, *Hands off.*

Who was she kidding? Yesterday in the conference room she'd been a willing participant. She was as much to blame for the lapse in judgment as Jonathan. And that's all it was—a lapse in judgment.

It wouldn't happen again.

She fastened her pearl stud earrings and nodded at her reflection. Then she slipped her Glock into its holster and locked her hotel room door behind her.

Today's rally was in a high school stadium. Though no venue could be secured completely, a stadium was preferable to others simply because it had basic security measures, like metal detectors, already in place. Abbie strode through the entry gates, examining the setup. On the other side of the chain-link fence were lines of people waiting to come in, even though the event didn't start for another hour.

She nodded at the uniformed security guards who stood at the gates, signaling that it was time to open them. Then she watched warily as the guards ushered people through the metal detectors, searched bags, and wanded the occasional person. Her security plan was only as good as the security team in place to implement it, and unfortunately, most of the security guards at the event were volunteers. They were probably more than adequate for a hometown high school football game, but Abbie was less than confident in their capabilities to respond to an actual threat.

Metal detectors were merely deterrents for minor criminals anyway. A criminal with the guts to go after a congressman in broad daylight would most likely have the means to bypass simple security protocols.

Which was why she'd be shadowing Jonathan's every move once he arrived.

She hadn't seen him since yesterday. It wasn't avoidance—there was just no reason to. He'd received a copy of the security plan, and she hoped she could assume that he'd bothered to read it.

So she kept a close eye on her watch and left the front gate ten minutes before Jonathan's car was scheduled to arrive. Her heels dug into the moist turf on the field as she crossed it to get to the back entrance.

His car was already there, idling. As she approached, he got out and buttoned his coat, looking more like an action-movie star in his dark reflective sunglasses than a politician.

Once again she cursed her luck in getting assigned to him rather than some potbellied, balding lawmaker. If that were the case, she wouldn't have to worry about her hormones going into overdrive every time she looked at her assignment.

He fell into step beside her, waving at the audience members with one hand and putting the other hand on the small of her back.

*Christ.* It was like she was walking with goddamn Miss America across the field.

The stadium was filling up, and people were standing directly in front of and around the stage set up at the visitor side of the fifty-yard line. She would have preferred people sit in the bleachers, which would have put some distance between Jonathan and the crowd, making it easier for her to keep an eye on things.

But Jonathan didn't want any distance—literal or metaphorical—separating him from the people.

*Distance*—that was something she was putting between *them* whether he liked it or not. From here on out she would maintain professionalism at all costs. Even if she did like the feel of his warm hand on the small of her back.

"You're early," she snapped, taking a few steps away from him so that he was forced to remove his hand from her back.

"Better early than late."

"You have to stick to the schedule. The security—"

He halted in the middle of the field and put a hand on her arm to stop her, too.

"Abbie, are you upset about yesterday?"

She was taken aback for a moment, not expecting him to address the elephant in the room so soon.

"No," she said curtly. "That's not what this is about."

He rocked back on his heels and crossed his arms, and she wished he'd take off those godforsaken sunglasses so she could see his eyes.

"Seriously," she said finally. "If you want to talk about it—"

"I didn't say I wanted to talk about it. I just asked if you were upset."

She narrowed her eyes at him. What kind of game was he playing? Politicians were good at those, but they weren't her thing.

"It was a regrettable mistake that won't happen again."

He stared at her for a beat, before resuming his progress toward the stage and remarking, "That's too bad."

She ignored his comment, not wanting to engage in conversation about it now. While he might be content to pepper her with innuendo, she preferred a more blunt discussion, and a political rally was not the place for the things she'd say.

She stepped up behind him on the stage. "Remember—if you *must* shake hands with the public when you're done, do it over there." She pointed to a designated corner of the field where people would be able to approach him from only one direction. With her at his side and two local police officers maintaining the crowd, Jonathan should be safe.

Or as safe as he could reasonably be, considering he refused to give up close proximity with his constituents.

Under Abbie's watchful eye, Jonathan bided his time on stage, chatting with the local government officials before taking to the microphone at precisely 2:00 p.m. He looked at her with one arched brow and tapped his watch. *Right on schedule.*

*What a prick.* Though she couldn't keep the small smile from playing at the edges of her lips. At least he was taking her advice—for once.

"Good afternoon," he said into the microphone. Abbie

tuned him out. She'd heard his speech a few times now—a bunch of political promises there was no way he could actually deliver. He might as well be promising world peace.

Although, Abbie recognized passion in his eyes and conviction in his words. He'd already done the impossible when he put legislation that had stopped more human trafficking in the last six months than in the last decade. Because of him, Hak Tanir was running scared. She guessed if anyone in Congress could fulfill promises, it would be Jonathan.

He was nearing the end of his speech, the part where he said the words he was famous for: "I hear you, and I'm here for you." She had to admit it was a catchy slogan.

Screams erupted in the back of the crowd, and they weren't the usual screams of exuberant women fawning over Jonathan. These were filled with sheer terror.

Abbie moved forward and put her arm across Jonathan's chest, pushing him behind her, while she scanned the crowd to try to figure out what the hell was going on. There were too many damn people.

It looked like a ripple went through the crowd, starting in the back, where people were shoving one another and running. Amid the screaming Abbie made out the word "gun."

She hauled Jonathan away from the podium and pushed him down the stairs toward two officers. Just underneath the stage was a bag she had stowed there earlier. She pulled out two Kevlar vests and tossed one to Jonathan. He shrugged into it, his eyes wide and his face pale.

"Go," she commanded her subordinates while she donned her own vest. "Get him out of here."

The officers flanked him and started to whisk him away, but he stopped, snapping out of his shock.

"Wait," he said. "What about you?"

Abbie pulled her Glock out of its holster. "I'm going to make that asshole wish he were dead."

Jonathan looked like he wanted to protest, but the officers pulled him away before he could get any words out. Abbie looked over her shoulder one last time to make sure they were sufficiently covering him.

Then she dove into the fray.

While everyone else was running away from the screaming people, Abbie ran toward them. Most steered clear once they noticed her gun, but she still took a few knocks from those running past, including one that almost caused her to fall on her ass.

It had been less than two minutes since she first heard the screams. The deeper she got into the crowd, the more panicked people were. Then she saw the blood.

A man lay on the ground, in so much blood that Abbie couldn't tell where it was coming from at first. A sobbing woman clutched at his hand and attempted to cover the wound in his stomach. With all the blood, Abbie wasn't sure it was doing any good.

She paused and knelt down to check his pulse. It was weak but steady.

"He'll live. Apply pressure here with both hands," she said to the woman, and then she pushed the button on her earpiece that connected her to the security team. "We've got wounded. Get the medics in here. Forty-yard line, home side."

She got to her feet again and spun around, still not sure where the gunman was. She was tall, but even with her height and her heels she couldn't see past the sea of people who battered against her in angry waves. So she pushed her way toward the place most people seemed to be fleeing from.

She encountered a lone man who wasn't panicking and was actually acting rationally. He was trying to direct people to safety in a fruitless attempt to maintain some sort of order.

"Where's the gunman?" she asked.

He rubbed his forearm on his forehead, leaving a streak of blood.

"Are you hurt?" she asked.

He shook his head. "Some people were shot over by the bleachers."

She didn't bother to ask how many or how severe the injuries were. Her priority was finding the threat and shutting it down.

"Where's the gunman?" she asked again.

The muted *thwap-thwap-thwap* sound of an automatic weapon firing was her answer.

"Get everyone outside the gate," she said before taking off again. That should be obvious, but she'd seen the unpredictable behavior that widespread panic caused. They'd be lucky if no one got trampled.

She moved toward the sound of the shots. Once she had visual confirmation, she took off running. There he was, thirty yards away at the edge of the crowd. He was wearing a full ski mask, of course, but she mentally calculated his stats. Around five foot ten. One eighty. Caucasian.

A shrill scream to her left caught her attention. It was a child—she'd guess no older than five—and he was down on the ground, getting kicked and stepped on in the frenzy.

She slowed, keeping her eye on the boy. Goddamnit, was no one going to notice him? A shoe connected with his shoulder, only narrowly missing his head. She made a split-second decision, diverting her course to scoop the boy up off the ground. She handed him off to the first capable adult, then spun back in the direction of the shooter.

*Shit,* where was he? *There.* He was retreating down the field at a sprint. Abbie dashed after him, her heels digging into the mud and grass, giving her traction on the slippery surface. She was closing the distance between them, but he still had at least forty yards on her.

When he got to the chain-link fence at the end of the field, he threw the gun over his shoulder and leaped up, easily scaling it. She got her first clean look at him, noticing the unusual bulk around his torso.

*The asshole.* She wasn't the only one wearing Kevlar.

Abbie took aim and fired, hitting the back of his upper

arm. He tumbled off the top of the fence and rolled a few feet, then jumped up and sprinted away.

"He's heading south," she said into her earpiece. "Male. Caucasian. Five ten. One eighty."

She allowed herself one last look at the perpetrator who had eluded her, before turning to help deal with the aftermath.

# Chapter 7

AS SOON AS Jonathan heard the shooter had left the stadium, he instructed his driver to return immediately. It killed him to be whisked away and wait in the safety of his car while the people were under attack.

Especially when they'd come to see him.

He opened the door before the car even stopped moving. His limited medical training was outdated, but he couldn't sit by and do nothing. Surely there was *something* he could do.

But what?

The parking lot was littered with police cars, ambulances, and fire trucks. People huddled together with shell-shocked expressions. Some were crying. Others were giving statements to police.

He was totally out of his element.

He started toward a group of distressed women who were standing together. The least he could do was provide comfort.

Instead he was met with a firm hand on his chest.

"What are you doing here?" Abbie asked.

He looked down to meet her gaze, and he noticed her fancy shoes were covered in grass and mud. They were ruined. There was a streak of blood on her cheek.

"Oh, God." He put his hand under her chin to tilt her face upward. "Are you hurt?"

She shook her head. "Nine people were shot. Two are in critical condition. There are quite a few minor injuries that occurred in the frenzy to get out."

He ran his hands through his hair, then left them on his head. *Nine shot, two critical.* All because of him.

*Christ.* And he'd cooperated with Abbie's security measures. Well, mostly. As much as he could. What would have happened if the shooter had come last time, when the venue was changed at the last minute and she was scrambling to put even the most basic of security measures in place?

He let out a shaky breath.

"How did this happen?" he asked.

"We're still putting things together, but it looks like he hid his weapon and several rounds of ammo in the stadium last night after our team swept for explosive devices. He came through the metal detectors empty-handed today, but since the seeds were already planted, he was able to execute his plan when he retrieved his stash from under the bleachers."

Her tone was matter-of-fact, but there was nothing matter-of-fact about this for him. Numbness set in.

"Miss Whitmore?" an officer asked. "The detective needs to see you."

She nodded, and he faded back into the crowd.

"You should go back to the hotel," she said to Jonathan. "There's no reason for you to be here. And it might not be safe. I was able to tag the shooter, but he still got away."

He blinked, and she came into sharper focus. Though her eyes were clear and her expression all business, she looked tired. Almost beat down.

"Are you okay?" he asked quietly.

"I'm fine." She frowned. "I already told you I had no injuries."

"That's not what I'm asking."

She took a shaky breath and her hard expression softened just a touch. "I've been better."

Then she turned on her destroyed heels, leaving him staring after her.

## Chapter 8

THE NEXT DAY Abbie sat across from Jonathan in his car on the way to the hospital. Though it would put him behind schedule for his next stop, he insisted on visiting the injured despite her attempts to convince him otherwise.

"So I guess your cover is blown, huh?" Jonathan said with a forced smile. "No one will believe you're just an aide now."

She nodded and looked out the window. In some ways that would make her job easier. She'd be able to call the shots without worrying about being discreet.

But she shouldn't have to worry about that at all. She should have had that asshole yesterday. Her fingers curled into a fist. She'd had visual confirmation, *damn it,* and she'd tagged him, but he still got away. If she hadn't had to stop for that kid, she would've caught the shooter.

She breathed slowly, trying to let go of her misguided anger. Jonathan was safe and no one had died. Those were the important things.

The car pulled up to the hospital, and she looked at the

squat stone building in trepidation. She'd been in her fair share of hospitals—after all, her job wasn't exactly a cushy desk job—but she'd never visited victims.

Victims she should have protected. She closed her eyes for a second, and when she opened them, her priorities were back in line.

*Jonathan.* He was her assignment. She couldn't save everyone.

But damn—she wanted to.

They stepped out of the car and were met by a police escort. Jonathan shook the officer's hand, and Abbie fell into step behind them.

The shooter hadn't been anywhere close to Jonathan. And now, while studying his stricken expression as they approached the first hospital room, she wondered if perhaps that was the point. There was more than one way to hurt someone. And this act of violence against the people Jonathan considered his had, in a way, wounded him—and deeply.

She hesitated at the door.

"Are you coming in?" Jonathan asked.

She shook her head.

He leaned close to her. "You saved them yesterday. You know that, right?"

She glanced into the hospital room, with its stark white walls a contrast to the bright arrangements of flowers and balloons.

"If I'd saved them, we wouldn't be here."

"That's not true."

"Congressman Lassiter! Is that you?"

Jonathan gave her arm one last squeeze before entering the room of the first victim on their list, an elderly woman who'd taken a bullet to the thigh.

Abbie watched from the doorway, telling herself she was standing guard, but she knew that was a cheap lie. If she came face-to-face with her failure, she'd lose all objectivity.

That was only part of the reason.

She used to be able to count on one hand the number of people who had been hurt under her watch. Now she needed three hands.

Logic told her that she was assigned to protect only Jonathan, but how could she see it that way when, in another room, a young mother of two was fighting for her life?

There had been two critically wounded, one of whom was the first man she'd seen on the field. He'd already been stabilized and moved out of ICU, but the young mother had taken a turn for the worse last night.

Abbie had tossed and turned all night after hearing that news. But there was nothing she could do about it now.

So she focused her attention on Jonathan, watched how he shook hands with everyone in the room, including the victim's twelve-year-old grandson. She expected he'd simply say hello and then move on to the next room, but instead he pulled up a seat. Ten minutes turned into twenty, then thirty.

*Damn.* He took his "I hear you, and I'm here for you" thing seriously. It wasn't just a line for him.

Abbie watched as he held hands with the elderly woman in the hospital bed and laughed at something she'd said.

Finally he stood and returned his chair to its original position. Before leaving, he once again shook hands with everyone.

When he came out, he smiled, but it didn't quite meet his eyes. "Ready for the next one?"

This had to be painful for him, but he was doing it anyway. And Abbie waited in the hall like a coward.

As they walked toward the next room, she slipped her hand into his, but kept her gaze straight ahead. If she didn't make eye contact, she wasn't breaking the cardinal rule, right? Out of the corner of her eye she saw him glance over at her with a surprised look on his face.

She squeezed his hand.

And didn't let go.

# Chapter 9

ABBIE WAS TIRED, but that didn't even compare to how Jonathan must be feeling. The usually talkative congressman hadn't said a word since their car pulled away from the hospital ten minutes ago. Instead he'd vacantly stared out the window.

Finally he turned to look at her. "Christ," he said, putting his fingertips over his closed eyes. When he opened them, Abbie saw they were bloodshot.

"You did a good thing here today, Jonathan." Abbie put a hand on his knee, not sure how to comfort him and a little unnerved that she wanted to.

"It's not enough. It's never enough. That damn Hak Tanir." He laughed bitterly. "Did you know it means 'righteous' in Turkish?"

Abbie nodded. She'd done her research on the human-trafficking group. Although they had originated in the Middle East, recent intel suggested they were now based somewhere in the States. They were fueled by a hatred of the US and a belief that women were inferior beings whose sole purpose was to serve men.

"Before you came, I met with the student body presidents from all the high schools and middle schools in the Hampton Roads area." Jonathan picked up a quarter from the floorboard and rotated it between his fingers. "I overheard a group of young ladies talking about Hak Tanir. They're afraid. After those girls were abducted in Chicago and Tallahassee, they don't feel safe. It sickens me that our young people have to worry about this sort of thing."

"I didn't realize you met with students."

"It's not advertised."

She cocked her head. "Why not? That would make for some great publicity shots."

"True, but that's not why I do it. The American young people are so disillusioned with our government. Voter turnout rates in the eighteen-to-twenty-nine group are at an all-time low. I'm hoping to change that. They need to be involved in choosing their political leaders. At least the president." He smiled wryly. "And if it gets me a few votes out of the deal when the time comes, that's a bonus."

Abbie had heard rumblings in Washington that Jonathan was being groomed to run for president when his party's incumbent finished his term in the White House. Of course, there were always rumors and gossip swirling around the capital, so she hadn't put much store in it.

"Are you planning to run for president?"

"That's no secret. I know it's a cliché, but I've been saying I want to be president of the United States since I was nine years old. The system may be slow and cumbersome at times, but it still works." He paused. "Mostly. There are a few areas that need improvement, and hopefully someday I'll be in a position to effect positive change."

Abbie studied him—his determined expression, his hand balled in a fist. Those words he spouted on the campaign trail weren't just words to him. He believed them.

His dedication was making her start to believe them, too.

And it was her job to make sure he stayed alive long enough to act on them.

# Chapter 10

"DO YOU WANT the last cookie?" Jonathan's hand was poised over the chocolate chip cookie in question.

Abbie narrowed her eyes at him. "What if I say yes?"

A pained looked crossed his face. "I'd be a gentleman and let you have it."

She laughed. No doubt he would.

"I'm stuffed. You take it."

He shoved the whole thing in his mouth. She'd like to say she was surprised, but having watched him house a huge salad, a steak dinner, cheesecake, and at least half a dozen cookies, she wasn't.

She *had* been surprised when he requested this meeting, though. Since it was last minute, they'd met for dinner in his hotel suite to strategize about the security measures at his next few events.

He slapped his hands together to shake off the crumbs, and their eyes met.

Clearing her throat, she broke eye contact and straightened her papers, ignoring the tingle that never seemed to leave her these days. "I think that just about covers it," she said, slipping her bare feet back into her heels before standing.

He rose as well. "Thanks for meeting on such short notice. I—" He paused and pulled his phone out of his pocket. "Sorry, I've been waiting for this text."

His lips slowly stretched into a smile as he read it, and when he looked up at her, he was beaming. "Samantha is out of surgery. It went well."

"Who's Samantha?"

"She's the mother with the collapsed lung."

Relief flooded over Abbie, and she closed her eyes for a moment. *She's going to be okay. Nobody had died.*

When she opened her eyes, she felt lighter. She'd put the injured out of her mind as best she could so that she could focus on her job, but they'd lingered in her memories from the shooting.

Jonathan put his fist in the air. "Yeah!"

Abbie chuckled at his exuberance, but she wouldn't fault him for his genuine involvement with the families affected by the shooting.

"This calls for a toast," Jonathan said. He rooted around in the minibar, coming up with a small bottle of wine. He squinted at the label. "Do you like…I don't even know what this is. Red? Do you like red wine?"

He grinned at her and held out the bottle. He wore his ever-present suit, but his jacket was off, several shirt buttons were undone, and his sleeves were rolled up. They'd started out the evening with the suit fully intact, but he'd soon ditched the tie, and it all went downhill from there.

But Abbie preferred him this way—a little rough around the edges, a little less than polished. He looked like an average man (well, definitely better looking than the average man) who came home from a long day of work to enjoy a beer straight out of the bottle.

She was tempted by more than just the wine.

"I should go, but you should celebrate." She picked up her discarded jacket and tucked it under her arm. Staying would be more than a mistake. She was glad they were finally on the same page regarding security measures, but anything more than a cordial working relationship would be too much.

For starters, it was unethical to engage in romantic interludes with clients. But that wasn't even her biggest concern.

It would be one thing if she were only attracted to him physically, but now Jonathan was someone she liked and respected. It was a slippery slope, and she could easily see herself sliding and developing actual feelings for him.

She'd already been down that road with her college boyfriend, and it had nearly destroyed her. The risk wasn't worth it.

But looking at his pleading eyes right now, she was tempted.

"Stay," Jonathan said. "Enjoy a glass of wine with me."

She was playing with fire, but damn if she didn't want to get burned.

"Just one glass."

His face broke out into an easy smile. "Excellent."

She sat on the edge of the sofa while he poured the wine into two glasses and handed her one. Then he sank down next to her.

"I'm still in shock about the shooting. I didn't think I was one of those 'it'll never happen to me' types, but I guess I am. And I wasn't even there for most of it, thanks to you." He raised his glass in a toast to her. "I don't know how you do it."

"It's part of the job."

Actually, it wasn't. It *shouldn't* be. If she'd been better at her job, it wouldn't have gotten to that point.

The truth was she'd done all she could reasonably do. The sad fact was that some people were hell-bent on causing destruction, and there was no way to stop all of them.

The only thing left to do was minimize the damage, and that's what she'd done. It was the only thing she could do.

She picked up her glass of wine, then took a sip and grimaced.

"That good, huh?" Jonathan chuckled and brought his own glass to his lips. He made a face, and for a moment Abbie thought the debonair congressman might actually spit it out.

"This is shit," he said. "I'm calling room service to get something better." He stood and walked over to the phone on the desk.

Abbie put her glass on the table. "No, I need to go, anyway."

He arched one brow. "What makes you think I'm ordering it for you?"

Abbie felt a flush rise to her cheeks, and she hurriedly stood and walked toward the door.

He beat her there, stepping in front of her to block the exit. She could smell the faintest scent of his cologne, and her belly clenched. She closed her eyes briefly.

She should step back, put some distance between them, but if she didn't leave right now, she feared she wouldn't ever be able to. So she reached around him for the door handle, but that only brought their bodies into contact, causing a fire to spark between them.

He put a hand on her arm. "Stay."

She looked up at him, and it was his eyes that did her in—those sharp crystal-blue eyes, which were now filled with longing, need, and so many things. Things that were probably mirrored in her own eyes.

Her pause gave him the moment he needed to cup his hands around her face and kiss her gently, not at all like the frenzied kisses they'd shared in the conference room. Without thinking, she reciprocated, wrapping her arms around his neck, dropping her jacket to the ground.

He ran his fingertips down her back, his touch light over the sheer fabric of her blouse. Her body reacted, her skin forming goose bumps in the wake of his touch.

She pressed herself more fully into him. He groaned and his touch become less timid, less gentle, and more urgent.

She pulled his shirt out of his trousers and yanked it over his head, not wanting to fool with the buttons this time. His skin was tan and taut, the ridges of his muscles evident.

His hands found her ass and lingered there. Then, before she realized what he'd done, her skirt was in a pool around her ankles. She stepped out of it and her shoes, kicking them both aside.

Her mouth found his again, though this time, with the new height difference, she had to pull him down to her first, and her hands moved over his belt buckle. Before she could get it undone, his hands cupped her ass once again and lifted her up, and she automatically wrapped her legs around his waist and ground herself against him.

"Not here," he said. "Bedroom."

He carried her in that direction, kicking the door open. Then he laid her out on the bed.

She propped herself up on her elbows so she could watch as he shed his pants and revealed his black boxer briefs.

"You are so sexy right now," he said hoarsely.

She looked down, trying to see herself as he did. Light-blue camisole, barely there black silk panties, long legs. She'd describe her body as capable, not sexy.

However, when he picked up her foot and kissed her ankle, all her nerve endings stood at attention. And as he slowly moved up her leg to her inner thigh, her back arched against the mattress and she threw her head back.

Now she felt sexy.

God, how long had it been since a man had touched her like this? The fact that she had to ask the question gave her an answer: *Too long.*

His stubble tickled the delicate skin of her inner thigh, putting a small smile on her face. Then the sensation was gone. She lifted her head up to look at him, and he held her gaze as he slipped one finger under the edge of her panties and pulled them down slowly, one inch at a time.

It seemed like it took minutes for the little black swatch to creep all the way down her long legs. All the while, a heat built steadily within her, urging him to hurry.

She wanted him, wanted to feel alive under him.

Before her panties landed on the floor, she lunged for him, grabbing his shoulders and pulling him against her so she could find his mouth. His hands skated up and under her camisole, along her sides to her breasts before he palmed them. Abbie broke away from him to pull her top over her head, and he made quick work of her bra, then threw it on the ground, next to her panties.

His mouth found her breast, and his tongue worked to harden her nipple while his hands moved between her legs. She fisted her hands in his hair—her back arched and she bit her lip. *Hurry.* She wanted more.

She attempted to slide his briefs down his thighs, but he soon took over and finished the job.

"Do you—"

He nodded, kissing her, not even letting her finish her

question. He hoisted himself off the bed and disappeared into the bathroom for a moment. When he returned, she was more than ready for him.

He crawled back over her, kissing his way up her body as he positioned himself between her thighs, his hardness pressing against her soft folds. Then he kissed her, slowly, gently, taking his time.

He pulled back to stare into her eyes as he entered her. When he seated fully within her, his eyes darkened and he groaned, resting his forehead against hers. She sucked in a breath as sensations ricocheted throughout her body, and she welcomed the invasion.

She pulled at his hips, working to set the rhythm. Pressure built inside her, and she let out a little whimper. The sound drove Jonathan on, urged him to pick up the pace, to grind against her clit with every inward stroke.

Her legs wrapped around him, and the shift in position sent tiny explosions through her.

She spread her hands across the flexed muscles of his back, digging her fingers in as the pleasure spiked, and the pressure built until, finally, she shattered.

His release followed seconds later, and he crushed his mouth to hers as he came.

# Chapter 11

THE SHARP KNOCKING at the door jolted Abbie from sleep, and she jerked, her hand searching fruitlessly for her weapon, the way it always did when she woke in a strange place.

She was used to sleeping in unusual places—that was part of the job. However, she was currently in a place that was stranger than most.

Jonathan's bed.

As a general rule, she didn't stay the night with a man. Especially a man she barely knew.

And never a man she was tasked with keeping alive.

She sat up as Jonathan answered the door. A hotel employee wheeled in a metal cart, complete with several covered dishes and the delicious smells that went along with them.

She closed her eyes and inhaled the sweet scent of cinnamon. *Mmm...French toast.*

Maybe she could stay a little while—at least through

breakfast. It would be rude to leave now, after Jonathan had gone through the trouble of ordering enough food to feed his entire staff, right?

She could rationalize it all she wanted, but the truth was she just wanted to stay—here, with Jonathan. If she wasn't careful, her perfectly constructed walls might start to lower.

Last night had been one of the best nights she'd had in a long time. The sex was mind-blowing, and it wasn't only because she'd been having a bit of a drought in that area. The congressman had moves.

Jonathan handed the woman some bills, and she gave a slight nod, then left.

"Good morning, sleepyhead." Jonathan's tone was teasing, and Abbie felt a blush rise to her cheeks. She wasn't the type of woman who blushed. And she wasn't the type of woman men wanted to make blush.

So what was it about him? Why did he make her fit into both categories?

Jonathan lifted the metal cover from one of the plates, causing the mouthwatering aroma of bacon to fill the air.

"Jesus, that smells good," Abbie whispered, closing her eyes and inhaling.

Jonathan chuckled. "My thoughts exactly."

He wheeled the cart toward the bed, and Abbie shifted to help, but then she realized she was still nude. She clutched the sheet under her arms.

"I got it," Jonathan said, setting up a tray on the bed. "I

wanted to treat you to breakfast in bed this morning. Something tells me you don't usually indulge like that."

"Or ever." Abbie snagged a piece of bacon and munched on it. Nice and crispy, just the way she liked it. She snuggled down in the covers, deciding to make the most of this rare extravagance. It was completely unprofessional, but professionalism had flown the coop last night.

Right along with her panties.

She might as well enjoy it.

Jonathan sat on the bed beside her. "Did you sleep okay?"

She nodded. She'd slept great. Nothing like a postorgasmic glow to knock a girl out for the night.

And what pleasant morning-after conversation. Of course, with all the women he'd dated, Jonathan must have had plenty of practice, she thought wryly.

She plucked a strawberry from the bowl of berries on the tray and forced her cynical side to tone it down. Most single men, especially ones who looked like A-list actors, had relations with the opposite sex. Just because her sex life had been lacking didn't give her an excuse to hold it against him.

She was about to ask him about his plans for the day—stupid question, since she already had his itinerary—when his phone rang.

"Sorry," he said with a grimace. "I should probably take that."

She nodded, and he stepped away a few feet.

"Barb, hi," he said. She was his personal assistant back in Washington. If Abbie's memory was serving her correctly—

and it always did—she handled most of his social agenda. Of course, in politics, business and pleasure often collided.

"Sandra Pensky for the Wentford dinner? Sounds good." Jonathan paced in front of the large picture window. Abbie was tempted to tell him to move away from it, but that was just her being paranoid. No one knew they were staying in this hotel, much less what room he was in.

"Can you also ask Vanessa if we can reschedule?"

Abbie's ears perked up. Could the Vanessa he mentioned be Vanessa Quinn, the notorious political socialite? Not that Abbie was into reality television, but Vanessa had made quite a name for herself on *The Real Housewives of D.C.* in the past few years. However, she was well known even before that, being the sole daughter in a family of American royalty that rivaled the Kennedys.

She'd divorced her husband, a senator, just last season after learning he'd cheated on her with another cast member. And now it appeared she'd moved on to greener pastures.

"I hate to cancel on her," Jonathan continued, "but I have a conflict that just can't be avoided." He shot Abbie an apologetic look and continued confirming dates while Abbie's mind reeled. It was like she was back in college again, being dumped for a woman with a better pedigree.

*No way.* Fool her once, shame on you. But she'd be damned if she'd be fooled twice.

She slid out of bed, holding the sheet around her, and gathered her clothes.

"Tell her I'll make it up to her, and pencil her in for lunch or dinner any day that I have an opening." Jonathan's back was to Abbie.

She slipped into her skirt and camisole, not bothering with anything else—she just needed to get out of there. Get out of there and be decent enough to get down the hall and back to her room for a long, hot shower, and try to forget the last twelve or so hours.

"Send her a bottle of Dom," Jonathan said. "That's her favorite."

Last night was a one-time thing. The shooting had seriously shaken her, and reassurance via sex was a natural human response to having escaped the crazy situation unharmed.

But it was something that wouldn't be happening again.

She picked up the last of her belongings and slipped out the door.

# Chapter 12

JONATHAN'S GAZE SHIFTED to Abbie the moment she stepped into the conference room. Not because she was obtrusive. No one else had even noticed her entrance. No, it was because he couldn't keep his eyes off her.

Last night had been…words weren't enough. And for him, a tried and true politician, that was saying something.

Women had come and gone in his life, but none of them had struck a chord that resonated with him like Abbie had. Though she was an enigma, she was someone he could see himself being with. She was his equal and rival in all things, challenging him in ways that no other woman had.

He had been sorry when his phone call ran long, and she'd had to leave. No doubt she'd slept in longer than she normally would have. That woman was on top of things and always in control.

Except when she'd been in his bed. He'd carefully stripped her of that control, and they were both better for it.

He lived his life by the "Work hard, play hard" mantra. It

was nice to have met someone who seemed to be willing to do the same.

He returned his attention to what Earl was saying, something about support for the Tallwood proposal. God, the woman made him lose his focus. It didn't help that his team had been sitting around this damn conference table for the last three hours.

"Earl, I'm sorry to interrupt you, but I'm famished. Is everyone ready for a lunch break?" At everyone's grateful nods, he continued, "Let's take a break for an hour, then reconvene this afternoon until I have to leave for that dinner."

He stood while his staff shuffled out of the room. Abbie was about to follow the last one out the door when Jonathan captured her wrist and started to pull her against him.

She disengaged her wrist and evaded his embrace, taking a few steps back. "I was going to update you on next week's itinerary, but it can wait until after lunch."

"That can certainly wait, but this can't." He wrapped his arms around her, but before he could touch his lips to hers, she put a solid hand on his chest.

"Jonathan, this is not appropriate."

"There's no one here."

"No, I mean this." She gestured between them.

Jonathan took a step back, letting his hands drop to his sides. Her face was masked and cold, not at all the face of the woman he'd spent the night with. She'd been passionate and open and sexy as hell.

An ice queen stood before him, shooting him a look so cold he almost shivered.

"What the hell?" he said.

She wouldn't meet his eyes. "We got caught up last night. It was the aftermath of the shooting. Emotions were high—"

"That's bullshit, and you know it." He put his hands on his hips. "That might have been part of it, but that wasn't all of it. Now, what the hell happened?"

"Nothing," she said, her back straight and her expression carefully neutral. The only thing that gave her away was the fire in her eyes.

"I'm calling bullshit on that, too."

"Look," she said sharply. "Last night was great—I'll admit that. But you and I don't mesh. We're too different. I'm not exactly the type of woman you could date or bring to a political function."

His thoughts went back to this morning, when he was on the phone with Barb. Shit, what must that have sounded like from Abbie's perspective?

"Everything you heard this morning was just work. I attend functions with those women to prolong my ability to network with them and other donors. Also because I don't have a steady woman in my life. It's business."

She snorted. "I've heard that story before." Then she closed her eyes and exhaled. "We need to keep this profes—"

"Something happened to you in your past. I can hear it in your voice. What is it?"

He knew they'd crossed a professional boundary, but her reasons for pulling back weren't because of her job. He was sure she probably bent a few rules to work in her favor regularly. No, this was personal. He could see it in her eyes, in the way she looked at him.

And damn if he was going to be brushed aside without at least knowing the real reason.

She leveled her gaze at him and opened her mouth, probably to spout out what was going to be another line, but then she sighed. "I dated a man in college—Matt Houser. You might know him. To make a long story short, I thought we were on the verge of engagement, when he dumped me and married a wealthy socialite only six months later. So I'll reiterate what I've said previously—your kind and I don't mix."

"My *kind?*" Jonathan stared at her, his mouth slightly agape. She'd put him in some damn category in her mind, with some idiot who thought she wasn't good enough. Why did that name sound so familiar? He snapped his fingers. "Wait a second. I know that guy. His father is friends with my father."

Her eyes didn't waver.

"But you already knew that, didn't you?" he asked slowly.

He'd visited Matt once or twice in college, but they'd lost touch over the years. Now he wracked his brain, trying to remember if he'd ever met Matt's college girlfriend. He probably had, but he just couldn't remember.

Or maybe he couldn't remember because he couldn't reconcile the woman across from him with a woman who'd dated that jerk.

"Matt's an asshole," he said simply. "I'm not like him."

Her expression told him she didn't believe him. To use his own words, like she was calling bullshit. But she'd be surprised, because he wasn't bluffing.

"Be that as it may," she said, "the fact remains that we need to keep our relationship professional. I crossed a line last night, and I don't intend to cross it again. I would call for a replacement, but I fear that leaving the campaign might seriously jeopardize your safety. So let's just try to make it to the end of your tour, shall we?"

The iciness in her voice and mannerisms was enough for him to stagger back a step. He wondered if he had any chance of melting the frost. Because, goddamnit, what they'd shared last night had been real. It had meant something.

But there was nothing he could do this moment to change her mind, so he smoothed back his hair and buttoned his suit jacket. "If you say so, Miss Whitmore."

# Chapter 13

THE PEOPLE SEATED around the dinner table laughed—
and not just the polite laughter afforded to the dinner host.
These were belly laughs. Some had tears rolling down their
cheeks. Other patrons at the tables around theirs had even
joined in—laughter really was contagious.

If Abbie weren't already so annoyed with Jonathan, she
might have found his little speech amusing as well. As it was,
all she could manage was a polite smile, and even that was a
struggle.

*Damn him.* Why did he have to make things so complicated? Her job was to assess the security risks and protect him
at all costs. And she couldn't do that if she was sleeping with
him—distracted by him. It was a clear conflict of interest.
She'd slipped up, and now she was trying to set things right
again. Why didn't he see that?

This seemed to be the only time in her life she'd actually
been grateful for her experience with that asshole in college.
Without it, she would probably have kept crossing that pro-

fessional line, which would potentially put Jonathan—and everyone else—in jeopardy. And all for what? To be cast aside in favor of a reality-TV personality who was made of silicone? No thank you.

No, she was doing the right thing, both professionally and personally.

She signaled the waiter for a refill of her water glass, wishing it were wine, which the rest of the dinner party was having. But she'd already crossed one line—she didn't dare cross another by drinking on the job.

The laughter died down and conversations picked up around her. She was seated next to an elderly woman who had been an early supporter of Jonathan's political efforts.

"You are so lucky to work with Mr. Lassiter at such a young age," the woman told Abbie. "I wish I had had that opportunity. Do you plan to go into politics yourself?"

"No," Abbie said curtly, then cleared her throat. She shouldn't take out her anger with Jonathan on this nice lady. "I'm actually not sure what I want to do, but all experience is good experience."

That was a line if she'd ever heard one. Seemed she was picking up a thing or two on this campaign.

Since Abbie was the only staff member attending the dinner, she'd gone under the guise of being his aide. There was no need to alert the guests to the extra security she was actually providing.

The woman patted her arm. "Very true. I worked in local

government for years, and I'd always planned to run at the state level, but then my grandbabies were born, and my priorities shifted, especially after my daughter's husband passed away."

Abbie leaned back so a server could clear her plate. Across the table several servers were doing the same.

One caught her eye. All of the other servers had waited on their table throughout the evening, but this guy was new. And there was something off about his uniform. She couldn't place it yet.

She smiled and nodded to the woman next to her, but she focused on the new server.

White top, black pants, maroon vest and bow tie, just like the others. But something was—*the buttons.* The buttons on his shirt were different.

She could just be acting overly paranoid, but in a five-star restaurant like this one, she didn't think they'd tolerate less than perfection.

And that bastard's eyes were shifty.

Their table was in a corner, so she stood, putting her back against the wall. "Just need to stretch my legs," she explained with a smile.

But really she didn't want the table to impede her if she needed to take action. She kept her eyes on the man. He was shorter than her, maybe five foot six, and a little on the pudgy side. Dark hair. Dark brown eyes. Mole on his left temple. Indistinguishable tattoo peeking out from under his shirt on his right wrist. She mentally catalogued everything about him.

He cleared the plate next to Jonathan's, his hands shaking as he set the dish on the tray, causing the silverware to rattle. A knife slid off the plate and onto the floor.

*That's it.* Her danger radar was wailing, and it wasn't just because he was horrible at busing tables. Something was not right with this guy.

She circled around the table toward where Jonathan was sitting. Without missing a beat in the conversation, he raised his eyes to hers, and the fury inside them was hot enough to light the whole room aflame. When he returned his gaze to the man on his left, his eyes were neutral again.

*Guess he's still pissed.*

But his feelings didn't matter right now. His safety did.

The suspicious server slipped his hand into his pocket, and Abbie quickly closed the distance between them. His eyes widened when he saw her approaching, and he backed up a step, upending the tray of dirty dishes.

Then he took off.

Abbie shot off after him, hurdling over the staff who had knelt to pick up the broken shards.

He darted between the tables, knocking over two patrons in the process. Then he pushed through an emergency exit, making alarms blare and lights flash.

Abbie followed him through the doorway, only steps behind. He wove through the cars in the parking lot. As Abbie's designer shoes slapped on the pavement, she simultaneously heard and felt the distinct snap of her heel breaking.

*Goddamnit!*

He was two strides ahead of her when he exited the parking lot to the sidewalk. However, if he crossed through the bustling traffic, she didn't know if she'd be able to keep up, hobbled as she was with only one heel, and he would get away.

*Not on my watch.*

She dove at him, tackling him from behind. He rolled, trying to buck her off him, but she used the momentum to keep him rolling until she had him facedown on the pavement again. She pressed her knee into his shoulder blade and brought his arm back at an angle she knew was painful enough to keep him immobile.

"What was in your pocket?" she demanded. When he didn't answer, she increased the pressure of her knee and used her other hand to push his face into the pavement. "What were you reaching for?"

He still didn't respond, and she sighed. They'd attracted a crowd—passersby who stood gawking. A man held up a cell phone with the intent to video.

"Don't you dare," she barked, and the man slowly lowered his phone.

She tapped her earpiece to request backup from her security team. They arrived within seconds, and she stood, hauling the man to his feet along with her. As they cuffed him, she reached into his pocket and pulled out a small vial with the tips of her fingers.

She held her hand out to the team. "I need a bag."

After bagging the vial, she inspected it closely but didn't recognize the contents. If she had to guess, she'd put money on its being some kind of poison, but she'd have to wait for lab results to be sure.

This spineless SOB wasn't the mastermind behind the plot to take out Jonathan. He'd turned and fled at the smallest sign of detection. *Damn.* She definitely wasn't undercover now. No doubt whoever was behind this threat would soon figure out her true reason for shadowing Jonathan.

But there was nothing she could do about that.

She glanced down at her shoes and sighed. This was the second pair she'd ruined on this assignment. But no way in hell was she switching to the orthopedic nightmares some of the older agents wore.

She hobbled back toward the restaurant with as much grace as she could muster, the heel on her left shoe dangling.

# Chapter 14

JONATHAN STARED ABBIE down across the living room in his hotel suite. They were both standing—she refused to sit, and he'd be damned if he had to look up at her to have this conversation.

"You caught the guy. So—"

"I caught *a* guy," Abbie interrupted. "Not *the* guy. There's no way that little prick is the mastermind behind all this. And he's lawyered up, so now we won't get anything worthwhile out of him."

"You want to monitor when I mingle, fine." He put both hands on the back of the couch and leaned, narrowing his eyes at her. "But cutting me completely off from my constituents is not an option. Not only will it hurt my campaign, but it's just not right. I won't be cowed out of this race."

She slammed her folder on the end table. "When are you going to learn that your safety is more important than your campaign?"

His nostrils flared as he took several deep breaths to control his anger.

The woman didn't get it. He didn't take his safety for granted, and especially not after the shooting that put several people in the hospital. But goddamnit, if he acted like his constituents were lepers and locked himself away, then Hak Tanir would win.

She, more than anyone, should know that the United States did not negotiate with terrorists.

He straightened and flashed his best politician's smile. "You're damn good at your job, Miss Whitmore. I think we both know that my safety—and that of my supporters—will be a problem."

That was a low blow, and he knew it. Maybe it would be enough to crack the hard exterior Abbie had developed. She'd avoided being alone with him since their night together.

And it irritated the hell out of him.

Why did he even care so damn much? She was a pain in the ass, and there were plenty of women—much more *pleasant* women—who liked spending time with him.

Too bad pleasant also meant boring.

"That's nice of you to say, but you're making it very difficult for me to do my job." Her tone was contemptuous.

*The job, the job, the job.*

Then a bitter thought crossed his mind—*It's like looking in a damn mirror, isn't it?*

"I'm sure you'll figure it out."

She looked him over in that scrutinizing way she always did. In the way that would make a lesser man break.

"I always do," she said smartly, then retrieved her folder from the table. Her heels click-clacked on the tile entry floor, followed seconds later by the slamming of his door.

Jonathan scrubbed a hand over his face.

*Christ.*

## Chapter 15

"NICE DAY, RIGHT?" Earl said brightly. *Too brightly*.

At first Abbie had been glad when he jumped into Jonathan's car at the last minute. She'd taken to sharing his ride for the last few events—in the name of security, of course. Varying in length, the commutes had all been tense and uncomfortable.

But now Earl seemed to feel the need to fill the silence with pointless chatter, which was only making things worse. She hadn't had enough coffee for this.

Abbie *was* good at her job. Jonathan's flippant comment was true.

But even though the last few events had passed without incident, they weren't technically victories for her assignment. Because then Jonathan thought he was right, and that she was being overprotective.

She wasn't his mother. She was a professional, and as a professional, she knew this wasn't over. No matter what Jonathan thought.

The man she'd turned over to security had died in custody. Suicide by poison was the official verdict. Maybe he'd realized that dying was better than dealing with his boss's wrath after screwing up his mission.

Or maybe that boss had taken him out. Either way, it didn't matter. The man's death meant that the threat to Jonathan's life was alive and well.

Their car pulled to a stop outside the construction site for the Rebecca Kreiger Library. The ground breaking was today, and Jonathan was one of the few who had been invited to wield a shovel. It was a large, open area, so while there would be security guards posted throughout, Abbie would be sticking close to him. He wouldn't be able to back up without stepping on her foot.

Which he'd better not. She was wearing new pumps and wasn't going to sacrifice another pair willingly.

As they crossed the parking lot toward the ground-breaking site, she tried to keep her vibe pleasant, while clearly broadcasting her RBF. She really didn't want to be distracted by having to make small talk.

Besides, small talk wasn't her thing.

She paused every time Jonathan did. He shook so many hands she itched to douse his in Purell. Thank God it wasn't flu season.

Once they arrived at the site, the event organizer handed Jonathan a shovel. Abbie stood behind him and off to the left.

"You may want to back up, miss," the foreman in a hard hat

told her. "I've been at a few of these, and you'd be surprised how some people fling the dirt behind them."

Abbie smiled tightly and took half a step back. Earl stood behind her with a few of the other staffers.

The mayor spoke for a few moments before turning the mic over to a middle-aged woman who was the quintessential librarian—white cotton shirt, plaid skirt, glasses, and a bun. She said a few words about the late Rebecca Kreiger. Then on the count of three the mayor, the librarian, and Jonathan dug in their shovels, to the delight of the cheering crowd.

A flurry of activity just behind Abbie caught her attention. Holly, the lone female on Jonathan's staff, was on the ground with her eyes closed. Her face was pale. Earl knelt next to her with a panicked look in his eyes.

"I think she was stung by a bee."

Abbie glanced at Jonathan, who was patting the shoulder of the mayor and posing for pictures. Then she glanced back to Earl. "Is she allergic?"

"I don't know…I mean, yeah, I think so. She's allergic to everything."

Abbie strode over and grabbed the woman's purse, then searched it until she came up with an EpiPen. She tossed it to Earl. "Here."

He looked at it like it was a grenade. "I don't…I can't…"

*For fuck's sake.*

She grabbed it out of his hands, tore the package open, and

removed the safety lid. Holding it in her fist, she brought it against Holly's thigh, mentally counting to ten.

Before she could start to massage the injection site, someone screamed. Abbie looked up sharply.

A knife was sticking out of the back of a man in a charcoal suit. He stumbled into the mayor, then fell to his knees.

*Jonathan.*

*Oh, God. No.*

People swooped in to help, and Abbie quickly lost sight of him.

She jumped up, and after she had ordered her subordinates to cover Jonathan, she followed the commotion and screams. That's where she'd find whoever had done this. Jonathan was already hurt. There was nothing she could do to fix that, but she would damn well find the person responsible and make him pay.

"Abbie! Abbie! There!" one of the staffers yelled at her, pointing toward the parking lot. "In the black!"

Half the people in the crowd were wearing black, but only one of them was running, shoving people out of his way as he went. That made it easier to pursue him—he'd already cleared the path.

He darted through the parked cars, in a replay of the other night at the restaurant, only this guy was much faster. He'd already made it to the neighboring shopping center parking lot.

*Shit.* If he had a getaway car waiting for him, she'd lose

him. The image of the knife protruding from Jonathan's back popped into her mind, and Abbie pushed for the extra speed in order to catch up.

She dove at the man, but something must have given her away, because he shifted to the right at the last second. She still managed to get a hold on his left leg, and they both went down hard on the pavement.

He kicked at her with his right leg, landing a blow on her shoulder.

*That's going to hurt in the morning.*

Though she still had hold of his leg, he managed to stand, shaking her off in the process. She clambered to her feet as he turned and ran, weaving through the cars in the lot.

*Dumb-ass.*

She took off in a straight shot, going around the row of cars and meeting him just as he emerged from behind a minivan.

She blindsided him, slamming him facedown onto the hood of a car. Quickly she pulled a zip tie out of her pocket and bound his hands. On his right wrist was a tattoo—in the same location as the faux waiter's tat.

"Who sent you?" she demanded. She flipped him over so she could look into his eyes, keeping her hand on his windpipe.

"You don't know who you're dealing with."

She threw a right hook, ignoring the flash of pain in her knuckles from the hit. He turned his head to the side and spit. It was laced with blood.

*Good.*

"Stupid bitch." He threw his head forward to head-butt her, but she was too fast for him, narrowly escaping the blow.

She pulled her gun and pressed it under his chin. "Try that again."

"You'll do what? Nothing."

She clocked him again, this time with her nondominant left hand. Even still, his head jerked to the side.

Remembering the onlooker who attempted to video her apprehension of the would-be poisoner, she knew she had to get this man out of the public eye. While she radioed for backup, she looked around for somewhere more private to continue this brief chat. Spying a construction trailer at the end of the parking lot, she hauled him that way.

By some miracle the door was open, and after pushing him through, she slammed it home and turned the lock.

"Who's trying to kill Congressman Lassiter?" She dug the barrel of the gun into his chin again.

When he didn't respond, she pistol-whipped him with the butt of the gun. "Who?"

"You won't shoot."

"Maybe not at first," she said with a serene smile. "First I'll break every one of your goddamn fingers."

She flipped him over and ground his face into the muddy carpet. She took hold of the pointer finger on his left hand.

"Who do you work for?"

"No one."

*Crack.*

"Goddamnit! You broke my finger."

And it had given her extreme satisfaction to hurt the man who had stabbed Jonathan.

Guilt, from not following traditional protocol, lapped at the edges of her conscience.

She dismissed it. This man had stabbed Jonathan. Her heart clenched. She refused to think about how bad the damage could be.

Because if she did, she would kill this piece of shit.

"Tell me."

"I don't—"

*Crack.* His words turned into screamed obscenities.

"You have eight more of those. Start talking."

# Chapter 16

JONATHAN WATCHED HELPLESSLY as paramedics loaded the librarian's husband into an ambulance. The man's blood was on his hands—literally and figuratively.

It was obvious the attacker had mistaken the librarian's husband for Jonathan. They were wearing the same color suit, were nearly the same height, and both had dark hair. From the back the mistake would have been easy to make. They'd even joked about matching each other before the ceremony began.

Jonathan accepted a rag from the project foreman and wiped his hands clean. Over his shoulder he noticed paramedics tending to someone else.

*Oh, no.* Another victim.

Abbie…where was Abbie?

His heart lurched into his throat, and he rushed to the scene.

But it wasn't Abbie. It was Holly, and Earl was with her. Holly was pale but looked to be all right for the most part.

There was no blood, anyway.

When Earl saw Jonathan, he stood and walked over.

"What happened?" Jonathan asked.

"Stung by a bee." Earl put his hands on his hips and shook his head. "She's severely allergic. Abbie got her with her EpiPen before she got too bad, though. So she should be fine."

"Where is Abbie?"

Earl shook his head. "She took off when the commotion started."

Jonathan strode toward the crowd, for once not stopping to chat with people and not giving a damn if that seemed rude. He wove through the people, looking for her and coming up empty. Near the parking lot he found one of her security team.

"Where's Abbie?" he demanded.

"I thought she was with you. She radioed for backup but wasn't there when we arrived, so we assumed she rejoined the staff." The man's confused expression caused fear and adrenaline to surge through Jonathan's veins.

Jonathan shook his head. "I haven't seen her since before the ceremony."

The man touched his earpiece. "Agent Whitmore, what is your location?"

Jonathan shoved his hands into his pockets to stop himself from ripping the man's earpiece out and screaming into it. What was taking so goddamn long? A madman was on the loose. *Where was she?*

She could certainly handle herself, but she wasn't infallible.

"Sir, she's not answering, but she was last seen heading toward the shopping center parking lot."

Jonathan took off in that direction.

"Sir! Congressman Lassiter!" the guard called after him, but Jonathan didn't stop or acknowledge him. Abbie would probably have words for him later about his taking off on his own, but he could think of only one reason why she would have left him unprotected, and it wasn't a good one.

There was no sign of her in the parking lot. Jonathan stopped and whirled around, looking in every direction. He tangled his hands in his hair and left them on his head.

*"Shit!"*

She could be anywhere. There was no one around, so he couldn't even ask if anyone had seen her.

Movement in the construction management trailer caught his attention. Maybe whoever was in there had seen something.

He knocked on the door, and when there was no answer, he tried to open it, but the door was locked. He heard what sounded like her voice, so he banged on the door.

"Abbie!"

Moments later he heard the door being unlocked, and much to his relief she stood just beyond the doorway—a little worse for wear but mostly the same as he'd seen her last.

But then he realized that steps away was a man with his

arms secured behind his back. His face was bloody and his hands were mutilated. His fingers were swollen and reset at odd, unnatural angles.

Jonathan swiftly surveyed the situation. It seemed his always-in-control protector had lost it. Something told him her detention of her prisoner was likely not sanctioned.

He couldn't blame her though. He wanted to kill the bastard himself.

Abbie's eyes focused on Jonathan and widened. Her arms slackened at her sides. She took a step toward him, then halted.

"How did you…I thought you'd been…" She broke off and put her hand over her eyes, unable to complete her sentence.

He closed the distance between them and took her in his arms. He kissed her temple, silently thanking God she was okay.

The guard Jonathan had spoken to earlier burst through the door, panting.

Jonathan quickly released Abbie. "She got him," he said to the security specialist, allowing Abbie the time to compose herself.

Abbie straightened, her eyes now clear and her expression level. "Take him into custody. Also please notify the EMTs that he has a few injuries that might need tending to."

"You stupid bitch!" the prisoner yelled. "I'm gonna sue you for this!"

The guard looked back and forth between Abbie and the man, no doubt putting the pieces together. Then he walked over to the man and roughly hauled him to his feet.

"You should be more careful the next time you try to assassinate someone," the guard said, leading him out of the trailer while the prisoner yelled obscenities.

Abbie took several deep breaths, her eyes on Jonathan.

He wanted to pull her to him again, to hold her and reassure himself that she was safe. But he knew she needed to collect herself.

"I thought you'd been stabbed," she said.

Jonathan shook his head. "It was the librarian's husband."

"Is he…" She trailed off.

"The paramedics were loading him into the ambulance when I left. I don't have any other information."

She looked over her shoulder to the place where the man had been lying only moments ago. "Shit," she whispered. "What did I just do?"

Jonathan no longer cared if his embrace would be welcome. She needed comfort, whether she knew it or not. He took her in his arms. While she didn't resist him, she didn't return the embrace, either.

"When I thought he'd stabbed you, I totally lost it."

"You're human," he said. "Mistakes happen."

She took a shaky breath. "I'm too emotionally involved. I need to step down."

"I don't accept your resignation." He waited for a small

smile or a smart retort telling him she didn't work for him. He got nothing.

She stepped away. "I need to think." Then she turned her back on him and walked to the door, pausing for a second but not turning around. "I'm glad you're safe."

Then she was gone.

# *Chapter 17*

ABBIE LET THE scalding water pour over her body, not even cringing as it stung her raw knuckles. She deserved the pain.

She'd given up her integrity to that asshole. She'd crossed another line. Had he deserved it? In her opinion, hell yes. But it wasn't her opinion that mattered here. That hadn't been her call to make.

And it was the reason behind her losing it that bothered her most of all.

*Jonathan.*

She couldn't deny it—she was developing feelings for him, and when she'd thought he was seriously hurt, she'd lost her shit. And that meant something. *He* meant something.

Now she needed to deal with that.

She turned off the water and wrapped a towel around herself. Standing in front of the mirror, she wiped a streak through the fog.

She'd gotten a scrape above her left eyebrow. Exactly when and how? She didn't know.

Had the hollowness in her eyes always been there?

She turned away from her reflection and grabbed her robe. Then she towel dried her hair until it was merely damp.

She tucked the essentials into the robe's pocket—earpiece, gun, room key—and opened the door.

It was a short walk to Jonathan's room.

Her hand paused before knocking on the door, and she took a few final deep breaths for courage.

But before she could knock, the door swung open. Jonathan stood there—no tie, the top buttons undone on his shirt, his hair disheveled. In his hand he held a glass of what appeared to be Scotch. His eyes were a little bloodshot and tired.

"I wasn't sure if you'd still be awake," she said.

Before she could talk herself out of it, she stepped into his room. She closed the door behind her and leaned against it, looking up at him and suddenly becoming all too aware of her nakedness under the robe.

He put his glass on a side table and used the tie from her robe to pull her to him. His mouth was on hers, devouring, while also feeding a need deep inside her.

She pulled his shirt out of his pants and undid the few remaining buttons. Her hands raked over his skin.

Her senses were on overload—the feel, touch, smell, and taste of him were too much. She'd been in his room less than a minute, and she already felt a fire building.

His hand snaked under her robe, and his fingers found her soft folds. She gasped as he stroked.

He took her up, higher and higher, until her knees went weak. The door against her back, and his arm around her waist, supported her.

"Jonathan," she said breathily.

Abruptly he stopped and stepped away. His eyes roamed over her body, the look in them clearly showing that he wanted her, not to mention his arousal, which was straining against his pants.

Why did he stop?

She clutched the robe closed, feeling completely exposed, body and soul.

"I can't do this again," he said hoarsely. "I can't be with you just to have you walk away."

She closed her eyes and concentrated on breathing for a few moments. When she opened her eyes again to stare into his, her heart rate had slowed.

"I'm all in," she said. "As much as I can be."

"Say that again," Jonathan said, wanting to make sure he'd heard Abbie correctly.

He stared at her, doing his best to think with the brain in his head instead of his dick.

But damn, that was nearly impossible with the way her damp hair hung around her face and the way she was looking at him with those sexy eyes of hers, no longer iced over. Not to mention the fact that she'd come knocking at his door wearing nothing but the white hotel robe.

To be precise, she hadn't actually knocked.

Truth be told, he'd been on his way down to her room when he found her standing in front of his door. He wasn't going to let her ignore what was between them any longer.

Now that she was here, though, he needed to be sure she understood what this meant. There would be no more distance between them. She meant too much to him for that.

He couldn't take being brushed aside again.

"I'm in," she said quietly. "But if we do this, I can't—I *won't* compete with other women."

"That's all you had to say. No more socialites, no more fake dates."

"But, Jonathan, I can't make any promises and—"

He didn't let her finish.

He cupped her face in his hands and kissed her, his mouth saying everything his words couldn't. There were no promises he could make, either, but he knew he needed her with him, at least for right now.

Though the kiss started gentle, it quickly progressed, growing hotter. It stroked the desire that was blazing in each of them.

She deftly undid his belt buckle, then set to work on his slacks.

He untied her robe slowly and slid his hands in the opening, gripped her ass and pulled her against him. She reached down to stroke the length of him, and he shuddered at her touch.

Her hip was pressed against the table beside the entryway, and he lifted her onto it, then stepped back for a moment to admire her. Her hands were flat on the table behind her, supporting her. Her long legs were parted, showing the delicate flesh at the apex of her thighs. Her pert breasts, with their pink nipples taut, rose and fell as she breathed deeply.

"You're so beautiful."

She closed her eyes for a moment, like she was absorbing the compliment. It shouldn't be like that—hard for her to believe. She should know how gorgeous she was.

He retrieved a condom from his pant pocket and quickly sheathed himself. Then he stroked her to make sure she was ready.

She was so wet.

She pulled him against her, leaving no doubt in his mind that she wanted him now. He settled himself against her and plunged forward. She gasped slightly before lightly nipping him on the shoulder with her teeth.

Then she wrapped her long legs around his waist, pulling him closer and deeper than he thought was possible.

His mouth found hers as his hips pistoned. He slipped his hand down between their bodies to press his thumb against her clit. She dug her fingernails into his back as she tightened around him.

Her pulsating muscles took him over the edge, and he groaned into her neck as he buried himself deeply within her one final time as he came.

## Chapter 18

SUNLIGHT POURED INTO the hotel room, dancing across the white duvet that Jonathan and Abbie were snuggled under. Both were awake, but there was no talking. Instead they curled up together, their need to be close unspoken.

Abbie trailed her fingertips along the light spattering of hair on Jonathan's forearm. She should get up. The morning schedule was clear, and she'd planned to go to the hotel's gym to make up for lost time. She'd be no good to anyone if she was too out of shape to chase the bad guys.

As Jonathan nuzzled her neck, her resolve weakened. She'd had a bit of a workout yesterday. Surely that counted for something, right?

Jonathan's phone rang on the nightstand. Abbie tensed, remembering what had happened the last time he took a phone call the morning after she'd stayed with him, but he made no move to pick it up and instead continued to trail lazy kisses down her throat and shoulder.

"Don't you need to answer that?" she asked.

"It can wait."

She moved to lie on her back, and Jonathan palmed her breast. She let out a contented sigh and ran her fingers through his hair.

*This is nice.* It shocked her to realize it. She wasn't the stay-in-bed-and-cuddle type. But she could definitely get used to this.

Except how would that work? Her job took her all over the country, and Jonathan's schedule was hectic at best.

"We should get moving," she said.

Jonathan sighed and sat up. "You're probably right. But just let the record show that you're the one who said it."

She sat up as well, tucking the covers under her arms. She nibbled on her lip. "What are we doing?"

"I have several conference calls…" He stopped as he turned toward her. "But that's not what you're talking about."

"No. You and me. What are we doing here? This doesn't make sense."

He shook his head. "No, it doesn't. But ignoring what's between us makes even less sense."

What he said was true, and besides, she didn't have it in her to fight it anymore.

She had a more important battle to fight—one to stop the attacks. There had never been any doubt in her mind that Hak Tanir was behind everything. And now her sources had confirmed it—the insignia that was tattooed on the right wrist of both men she'd captured had been identified as a symbol for the group.

But confirmation that the human-trafficking organization was behind this didn't answer her most important question—how were they getting their information? Sure, Jonathan's schedule was public knowledge, but they seemed to have an inside track.

There was a knock at the door, and Jonathan rose to answer it, slipping into a pair of pajama pants.

"Do you have an appointment this morning?" She had thought his schedule was clear.

"Room service," Jonathan said. At her frown, he grinned. "I woke up in the middle of the night, so I put in an order."

While Jonathan dealt with their breakfast, Abbie put on her robe. Coming down here without a stitch of clothing was probably not her best idea.

Jonathan was closing the door as she entered the living area. She looked gleefully at the room service cart, hoping the spread would be comparable to last time. If the delightful aromas were any indication, it would be.

Her stomach growled. She'd lost her appetite last night after everything that had happened, and she had skipped dinner. Now it was back with a vengeance.

Jonathan lifted the cover off a basket to reveal croissants. In his other hand he held a plain white envelope.

She inclined her head toward it. "What's that?"

"It was included with the hotel's daily itinerary."

Abbie stopped chewing the piece of croissant she'd just bitten off. Her mouth had suddenly gone dry. "Open it."

Inside was a plain white sheet of paper with plain type. He grimaced as he read, then held it out for her to see.

*Stop hiding behind the woman. She's only good for one thing. The third time's the charm. See you soon.*

Jonathan's hand tensed and his fingers gripped the paper like he was about to ball it up.

"No," she said, holding it by the corner. "We need to take this into evidence."

"There's more," he said grimly. He reached into the envelope and pulled out a single photograph. In it were several girls in various stages of undress sitting on a filthy bed. There were bruises and abrasions on their skin. These girls were victims of the human trafficking that Jonathan had fought so hard against.

And they couldn't have been older than fourteen.

Abbie put a hand over her mouth, but a strangled cry still escaped. She'd heard about the atrocities being committed, but she'd never actually seen a photo. In her line of work she'd seen some messed-up stuff, but this hit her hard.

Jonathan grabbed his Scotch glass from last night off the table and threw it against the wall, the sound of the shattering glass breaking the silence. Then he sighed and placed the picture facedown on top of the letter.

"This," he said quietly. "This is why it's important for me to go on. Someone has to fight against this. Someone has to stand up to them. Even if I cancel just one event, I feel like I'm letting them win."

Abbie put her arms around Jonathan. "I know. But I don't want you getting hurt, either."

She eyed the white back of the picture. Though it was face-down, the heartbreaking image was burned into her memory.

# Chapter 19

JONATHAN TAPPED HIS fingers on his knee in his car, then sighed and looked at his watch. He was late. He *hated* being late. Timeliness was such a small thing, really, but it said a lot about a person's character.

And now because Abbie had insisted on a last-minute venue change, his driver had gotten mixed up. Even if they hit every green light, they'd still be at least ten minutes behind schedule.

Her hand reached for his and quickly squeezed before letting go. "Thank you for not fighting me on the change."

"I trust you," he said. "And I don't want anyone else getting hurt."

She nodded.

"You still haven't told me why you wanted to change the dinner location, though."

"Hak Tanir sending you that note shows they're getting reckless and impatient. I'm testing out a theory."

"Are you going to share that theory?"

Her tightened lips gave him the answer. He sighed and resumed tapping his fingers on his knees.

*You trust her,* he reminded himself. But it was hard not to be annoyed at being kept in the dark. He liked to be in control.

The car finally pulled up to the restaurant, and someone was waiting to escort him to the private room where he'd be meeting his biggest supporters in the Richmond area. Most of them were wealthy business owners. He valued both their donations to his campaign and their insight into the local economy.

Abbie stood with her back against the wall, observing. Every so often he'd feel her gaze on the back of his neck, and he'd start thinking about things that were highly inappropriate, considering his current company.

*Damn.* He enjoyed dining with his supporters, but he might just have to have his dessert back at the hotel.

With Abbie. Naked.

Her presence made it hard to concentrate on the conversation around him, which was a first.

After dinner they lingered over coffee, and he kept checking his watch. When the last guest finally called it a night, he threw his napkin on the table gratefully and headed toward Abbie.

"You must be tired from standing for hours." He looked down at the high stilettos she wore. They were sexy as hell, but they sure weren't practical.

She shrugged. "Not really. I'm used to it."

He buttoned his jacket and put his hand on the small of her back to guide her out to the car. "I guess your theory didn't hold up," he said. "No incidents. Don't get me wrong. I'm not disappointed about that or anything."

He held the door open for her and waited for her to walk through it.

Instead she sharply inhaled and flung her arm around his shoulder, pulling him to the ground.

The glass door shattered behind them, showering them with shards of glass.

"Shit!" Abbie said.

"Go," he said. "I'll take cover in the car. There's another security guard there."

She spared him a side-eyed glance before making her way outside.

Now it was his turn to curse.

He didn't like this. Not at all. The primitive part of him was protesting that he should be the one taking the risks to catch the bad guy while she remained in safety.

But she had skills he didn't.

The restaurant manager rushed over to him before he got in the car. "Sir, are you okay?"

"Fine," Jonathan said, brushing the glass off his jacket. He stood as close to the door as was safe to do, trying to catch a glimpse of Abbie.

"And your lady friend?"

"She's fine." Except was she? She was out there chasing down a shooter. She knew what she was doing, but anything could happen.

He was still standing at the door with the manager when the first police cars pulled up minutes later, their sirens blaring.

Abbie walked back onto the scene just as the officers were getting out of their cars. Tension left Jonathan's shoulders as his eyes met hers.

*Thank God.*

Judging by her expression, the shooter had gotten away, and she was pissed.

But at least she was safe.

# Chapter 20

ABBIE LEANED FORWARD to bite into the piece of chocolate cake Jonathan offered on his fork. She closed her eyes as she chewed.

Her taste buds almost had an orgasm.

"This is so good." She licked her lips.

"Let's order another slice," Jonathan said.

She shook her head. "It's so rich. I don't think I could have more than a few bites anyway."

Abbie took the napkin off her lap and moved to the sofa so as not to be tempted by the cake.

If she'd been asked a month ago if she'd be sharing cake with Congressman Lassiter and lounging in his suite in yoga pants after thwarting an attempt on his life, she'd have bet money against it.

But after dealing with the local police, they'd returned to the hotel and Jonathan had immediately ordered room service dessert, even though it was almost two in the morning. She was pretty sure the kitchen was closed, but somehow, twenty

104 · JESSICA LINDEN

minutes later, a hotel employee had come knocking with the aptly named Death by Chocolate cake.

"Will you tell me your theory now?" Jonathan asked, joining her on the sofa.

"Fine," she sighed. He wasn't going to like hearing this. "There's a mole on your staff."

Jonathan's eyes widened, then he frowned. "Are you sure?"

"It's the only explanation. Your staff are the only ones who knew about the venue change. It wasn't a public event, so it wasn't advertised. Someone has to be passing along information."

Jonathan rubbed his chin, and his brow furrowed. "Do you have any idea who?"

She shook her head. "I don't know them well enough. But I have my intelligence team diving deeper into everyone's background, and I'll be getting to know them very well in the coming days." She paused. "If you had to guess, who would it be?"

He looked away. "I don't know."

His distraught expression was the reason she hadn't told him about her theory earlier. It obviously tore him up to think that someone he worked with on a daily basis was an accessory to several attempted assassinations. A traitor. She hoped she was wrong, for his sake.

But this was the first real break she'd had. Since she'd been assigned to this case, she'd been on the defensive. And that was fine while the threats were only that—passive threats. Now, though, Hak Tanir was getting more and more aggressive.

It was time to go on the offensive.

There was a break in between the events on his tour, and most of his staff members had traveled home to spend the time with their families. Abbie and Jonathan had opted to stay put. Neither had anyone to go home to, anyway.

With the lull in events, it was the perfect time for Abbie to set up a trap.

Part of the reason Jonathan was still alive was dumb luck. Though she was one of the best bodyguards the Cartwright Agency had, the odds weren't in Jonathan's favor. With the number of attempts on his life, he *should* be dead now.

Soon enough Hak Tanir would tire of the failed attempts. The note and picture proved they were getting to that point already. They were going to step up their game soon.

And she'd be ready and waiting.

## Chapter 21

ABBIE PUT DOWN the phone and stared at it like it was suddenly dangerous and contagious. Had she really just endured a twenty-minute conversation on the different varieties of syrup? Maple, low-sugar, strawberry-flavored, the list went on and on, and now Abbie knew far more than she'd ever wanted to know.

Was there any way she could get those twenty minutes of her life back?

She just shook her head and checked the item off her list. When she took this job, she'd had no idea she'd turn into an event coordinator, but that's exactly how she'd spent the last several days.

*Christ.* She scrubbed a hand over her face. She was totally out of her element, but she certainly couldn't turn these tasks over to Jonathan's staff—not when it housed a traitor. No, she wanted to control every little detail.

She'd be glad when Juliet, a fellow agent from the Cartwright Agency, arrived tomorrow. It didn't pain her one bit to admit Juliet was better at these sorts of things. Each agent had her specialty, and domestic affairs was not one of Abbie's. Her strengths lay in security assessment.

Jonathan came into the room and smiled wryly at her expression. Without a word, he stepped into place behind her to rub her shoulders.

Abbie rolled her neck back and groaned as he worked on a particularly tight spot. "You're lucky I like you," she said.

He leaned down and kissed her temple. "That may be true, but even if you didn't, you'd still do your job and do it well."

She grunted in response. He understood her, and she was still getting used to that fact.

"Are you sure you won't actually cancel your remaining events and save us all the trouble?" she asked.

When Jonathan immediately stopped massaging her shoulders, she sighed. "That's what I thought."

He sat across from her at the little dinette table in her suite that was serving as her temporary office. *Damn.* She should have kept her mouth shut. Her shoulders were already tensing up again.

Not that she didn't care about everyone she was tasked to protect, but she'd be lying if she tried to deny that she cared about Jonathan more.

"I don't like lying to my staff."

She narrowed her eyes at him. "You know why—"

He put his hand up to stop her lecture. "I'll do it, but I don't like it."

She touched his arm, saying nothing. He still didn't want to believe that one of his staff members was selling him out, but he wasn't stupid, either. After the last incident it was the only logical answer.

Jonathan checked his watch. "Shall we go? They should already be in the conference room."

Abbie nodded, tucking her papers neatly into a folder.

As Jonathan had anticipated, the staff members were already gathered in the hotel conference room, back from the week-long hiatus.

Earl smiled when they entered, and opened a huge box of doughnuts. The scent of sugary glaze filled the air. "Welcome back, sir."

Jonathan clapped the other man on his shoulder. "Thanks, Earl. I hope you had a nice break."

Instead of sitting at the head of the table as he normally did, Jonathan remained standing. Abbie stood at the other end of the room, where she had a clear view of him and everyone else.

Jonathan cleared his throat, and the staffers took their seats. "There's been a change in plans."

Everyone looked up at him with their pens poised over their notepads and confused expressions on their faces. Abbie could sympathize. Jonathan rarely changed his itinerary once it was set, which had been a point of consternation between them for the last month.

"I can't, in good conscience, put anyone else at risk." He

paused, an appropriately troubled look crossing his face. "I'm canceling the rest of my tour dates."

His announcement was met with a brief moment of silence and shocked expressions.

"What?" Earl exclaimed, a vein popping in his forehead. "You can't do that!"

Beside him, Holly started coughing. The staffer on the other side of her frowned and said, "Oh, crap. Some of those doughnuts had peanuts on them. You didn't get one of those, did you?"

"I should be fine," Holly said, but her face was pale. "If you'll excuse me, I need to grab some medicine from my room."

"Not a problem," Jonathan said. "I apologize for the change in plans, everyone, but it's the responsible thing to do."

"With respect, sir, I disagree." Earl crossed his arms and shot Abbie a dirty look. "You can't back down. That's what they want."

"I agree, Earl. Trust me, I agree. If I were the only one at risk, I would proceed as planned. But I'm not. Innocent people have been shot and stabbed at my events. It's a miracle no one's been killed."

Earl said nothing but continued to glare at Abbie. She leveled her gaze at him until he looked away. She'd known the staff would hold her responsible for the cancellation, but she didn't care.

"The cancellations aren't public knowledge yet," Jonathan

said. "It's a sensitive issue, so I'm still determining how I want to break the news, but I wanted to let you all know first. In the meantime, Miss Whitmore is planning a pancake breakfast fund-raiser for early next week. The proceeds will benefit the victims from the shooting. It will be my last public appearance for the foreseeable future."

The truth was there would be no proceeds—Jonathan was footing the bill for the whole thing and donating a sizable sum of his own money. The attendees at the breakfast would consist of Cartwright agents, police officers, and military personnel. Basically, everyone Abbie could scrounge up who could handle the situation.

Because she was betting on the traitor leaking this information to Hak Tanir. As far as they knew, it would be their last chance to strike against Jonathan. They'd take her bait. And then Abbie would take them down.

## Chapter 22

JONATHAN SWIRLED THE wine in his glass, staring into it. He and Abbie were having a room service dinner in his suite, and even though the steak was top quality, he was having trouble choking it down.

Across from him, Abbie laughed. "Relax. Your staff will forgive you for lying to them." She paused. "At least, the innocent ones will."

Jonathan set down his wineglass and sighed. She had him pegged. He understood that strategy sometimes required less-than-honorable means, but he didn't have to like it. His staffers were some of the most loyal on Capitol Hill, and he hated damaging that trust.

"Do you have a short list for the traitor yet?"

This time it was Abbie's turn to scowl. She angrily poked at the steak on her plate. "No," she admitted. "Earl is the only one who protested the change. No one else seemed particularly bothered by it, but I don't think it's him. Frankly, he's not savvy enough."

Jonathan frowned. Earl was a good man, and Jonathan didn't know what bothered him more—the fact that Abbie had considered Earl or the fact that she'd dismissed him for lack of intelligence.

She put her silverware down on her plate with a clang. "I'm missing something, and damn it, I can't figure out what it is. All of your staffers check out. None of them have any kind of tie, not even a small one, to any shady organizations, and trust me, I dug deep. Your staffers are squeaky clean."

At that Jonathan smiled. He could have told her that. He'd done his homework before hiring them. Or at least, his trusted assistant back in Washington had.

"The most risqué thing I could find was on Mark," Abbie said. "A drunk-in-public citation on his twenty-first birthday."

Jonathan knew that already, but it wasn't the sort of thing he'd hold against anyone. Hell, he was lucky he hadn't ended up on the wrong side of the law during a few rowdy nights in college.

"What's the craziest thing you've ever done?" Jonathan asked. Abbie blinked, seeming surprised by the change in subject, but Jonathan was tired of talking about Hak Tanir. He had faith that Abbie would figure it out, and in the meantime, he wanted to make the most of his time with her.

Because once the situation was resolved—and with Abbie on the case, it would be soon—there would be no reason for her to stay on his tour. Neither one had acknowledged that fact.

"Well, there was this one case where—"

Jonathan shook his head and held up his hand to silence her. "Something crazy that Abbie did. Not Agent Whitmore."

She furrowed her brow. "I'm not really the crazy sort."

Jonathan settled back in his chair and picked up his wineglass to wait.

"Okay, fine." She removed the napkin from her lap and dropped it on her plate. Then she pushed the plate away and rested her arms on the table. "When I played soccer in high school, my teammates and I snuck into the rival team's locker room the day before a big game."

"Let me guess. You stole the mascot."

She shook her head. "No, we didn't steal anything. We simply…relocated some things."

Jonathan laughed at her rationalization of what was probably a harmless prank from over a decade ago. "Tell me more, Agent Whitmore."

"We put their uniforms in the freezer." A slight blush crept onto her cheeks, and Jonathan tried to imagine a teenage Abbie—a slightly dorky, more carefree Abbie. She was still in there, buried deep below the serious, badass agent. He hoped to get the chance to dig her out and get to know her—another side of his Agent Whitmore.

He reached across the table and took her hand, then pressed his lips to it. "You were such a deviant."

She cleared her throat, the blush gone. "It was a silly prank.

I should go. I need to review some things before Juliet's arrival tomorrow."

"Of course," Jonathan said. "I have some phone calls to make as well. But after?"

Abbie's eyes darkened and her lids lowered ever so slightly, causing Jonathan's gut to tighten.

"I'll come back," she said simply.

# Chapter 23

THE WORDS BLURRED on the page in front of her, so Abbie rubbed her eyes. She'd found nothing new. Two hours had been wasted.

She pushed the files across the table as far away as they could get, then capped her pink highlighter and flung it across the room.

No one could be as innocent and virtuous as these people, especially no one in politics. Where the hell had Jonathan found them? Earl was a freaking Eagle Scout.

She opened her laptop. Despite her blurry vision and her brain pounding against her skull, she wasn't giving up. Not yet. Everyone made mistakes. She just needed to find the slipup that would reveal who their traitor was.

She scrolled through the staffers' profiles on various social media sites, scrutinizing every post, every comment, every photo, until she thought she'd scream. If she had to look at one more picture of Earl's parakeet, she just might.

Holly's Facebook page was similar—lots of pictures of her

cat. Who was taking care of the cat now? Holly had been on the road for over a month.

And why was Abbie even thinking about that? She shook her head. It was a definite sign that it was time to call it a night. Well, maybe not quite yet.

Heat pooled in her belly at the thought of climbing back into Jonathan's bed.

She had put her hand on the laptop screen to close it when a picture caught her eye. It was Holly and her younger sister. The girl looked vaguely familiar.

But then again, after all the pictures she'd seen on Facebook this evening, *everyone* was starting to look vaguely familiar.

But still, she paused, looking closer at the picture. Her gut told her she'd seen this girl before.

And her gut was never wrong.

But she hadn't seen her in person or even online. No, it had been in a photograph, a printed one. She didn't have any printed photos of anyone but the staffers and—

*The picture that had come with the threatening note.*

Abbie jumped out of her chair to retrieve the files she'd pushed away. She hurriedly flipped through the papers until she had a copy of the picture in her hand.

She held it next to Holly's sister's picture. Hannah had turned eighteen three months ago. At first glance the girls in the picture had looked young to Abbie. Strip Hannah out of her makeup and trendy clothes, though, and with her baby face, she could pass for fourteen.

Hell, she *had* passed for fourteen. Abbie would've sworn the girls in the picture were no older than that. And she usually wasn't wrong when it came to guessing ages.

So unless Hannah had a doppelganger, Holly's little sister had been abducted by Hak Tanir.

Which meant Holly was the mole.

# Chapter 24

JONATHAN PROPPED HIS phone on his shoulder to free his hands to hang his recently dry-cleaned suits in the closet. He wrinkled his nose at the sharp chemical smell. He couldn't wait to get back to Washington, where he could have his suits cleaned at his regular shop.

"Have you thought about who you might want to run with?"

Jonathan forced himself to pay attention to what his father was saying. It was late, almost midnight, but his father had always been a night owl.

"I have a few people in mind," he said vaguely. There was silence on the other end of the line as his father waited for him to elaborate. The senior Mr. Lassiter had also been in politics, serving two terms as the governor of Virginia.

"I'm not ready to discuss it," Jonathan said finally. "It seems a bit premature."

"It's never too early," his father admonished. "Now is not

the time to be modest. Everyone in the party knows you're our best bet for another eight years in the White House."

"Not everyone."

His father chuckled. "No, of course not everyone. But everyone who has any sense, anyway."

Jonathan yawned, covering his mouth with his hand too late.

His father chuckled again. "You're tired. I'll let you go. But, son, I'm proud of you."

"Thanks," Jonathan said, the same response he gave whenever his father said that, which was every time they disconnected from a call. He knew his father wasn't just saying that. His father had devoted his life to public service, and he'd been delighted when Jonathan followed in his footsteps.

The apple hadn't fallen far from the tree.

Jonathan tossed his phone on the dresser and rubbed his eyes. *Just another month.* He'd never admit it to anyone, but he was ready for this tour to be over.

It pissed him off. He normally loved meeting with his constituents. Just another reason to hate Hak Tanir.

Soon it wouldn't be an issue. He knew that Abbie would get the case wrapped up in the next few days.

A knock sounded at his door, and his lips teased into a smile as he crossed the room toward it. *About damn time.*

Abbie was the best thing to come out of this experience. He would never have met her otherwise. She was a complicated woman—all business in her black suits but wearing black lace lingerie underneath. And then there were her fuck-me heels.

So many layers, and he enjoyed peeling them back.

He opened the door with a smile. "I was wondering…" The smile fell off his face, and he silently cursed himself for breaking the easiest damn security protocol—looking through the peephole before opening the door.

"*Shit.*" He tried slamming the door, but in his exhaustion his reaction was delayed and he was easily overpowered.

*Abbie's never gonna forgive me for being so stupid* was his last thought before everything went black.

# Chapter 25

ABBIE POUNDED ON the hotel room door, not caring that it was after midnight. *That bitch better answer.*

Within seconds, she heard clumsy footsteps on the other side of the door, but it remained closed.

Abbie's already thin patience was almost shredded.

"Holly, I'm coming in there one way or another, so you might as well open up now and save me some trouble." She paused. "Save yourself some trouble, too. Do you know the penalty for impeding a federal investigation?"

After a few seconds the chain on the other side of the door rattled.

Abbie wasn't exactly conducting a federal investigation, but Holly didn't know that. And in any case, Abbie had the power to make her life hell until she cooperated.

Holly flung open the door. Her eyes were bloodshot, and her clothes looked like they'd been run over by a Mack truck—while she was still wearing them. In one hand she clutched a plastic wineglass that was missing its bottom.

Abbie pushed past her into the room, slamming the door closed behind her. There was no need to give the entire hall an earful.

She held up the picture of the young girls. "Tell me about this picture."

Holly's eyes widened, not in surprise but in recognition. The plastic wineglass slipped out of her hand, dropping to the floor. Wine splashed on Abbie's shoes, but she kept her stare trained on Holly's face.

Holly threw up her hands, letting out a strangled cry.

"Talk," Abbie demanded, her tone angry. Perhaps she could be a little gentler with the distressed woman, but Holly had recognized that picture. She'd known about it and hadn't said anything.

Holly moved her hands away from her tear-streaked face, sucking in breath like she was choking.

That was all Abbie needed—for the woman to pass out on her. She scanned the hotel room, spying an inhaler sitting on the table next to the boxed wine. She grabbed it and held it out to Holly, who stuck it in her mouth and inhaled deeply.

"Now talk," Abbie said, careful to keep her tone even.

"That's my sister."

"You've seen this picture before."

Holly nodded, then crossed the room to sink down onto the couch, her hands clasped between her knees. "Can you put it away? I...I can't stand to look at it."

Abbie laid the picture facedown on the table but didn't join Holly on the couch.

"Hannah is ten years younger than me. She was unexpected—a late-in-life baby for my parents, and they spoiled her rotten. It wasn't a big deal until she was fifteen. That's when she ran away the first time." Holly paused, her gaze focused on the carpet.

"So she ran away more than once?" Abbie prompted.

"Yes." Holly remained fixated on the carpet, not looking at Abbie. "I couldn't even tell you how many times. It was so many my parents stopped reporting it. The last time she didn't come back. Although my parents were concerned, they were just so tired of it. They figured she'd come home when she was ready. And since she was eighteen, they wouldn't get in trouble for her truancy. But then about a month ago I got that." She nodded toward the picture.

"Just the picture? Anything come with it?"

"A letter."

"Was it sent by e-mail or regular mail?"

"Regular mail."

Abbie ground her teeth, waiting for Holly to elaborate. "What did it say?"

Holly looked up at her with wild deer-in-the-headlights eyes. Her chin quivered.

"Holly, what did the letter say?" Abbie braced herself for an answer she knew she wasn't going to like.

"I had to do it. They were going to kill her."

Abbie closed her eyes for a moment. "You realize that you have the ear of one of the most important congressmen in the country. Jonathan would have helped if you had told him."

Holly shook her head, tears streaming down her face. "They would have killed her."

"What did you do?"

Holly clamped her mouth shut, squeezed her eyes closed, and shook her head. "No, no, no, no."

The hairs on the back of Abbie's neck stood on end. It didn't take a genius to figure out that Holly had fed information to Hak Tanir. But there was something else going on here.

"Holly," Abbie said, her sharp tone demanding attention. *"What did you do?"*

"He canceled the events. I had to tell them."

Abbie grabbed Holly by the shoulders and shook her, forcing her to look into Abbie's eyes. "What did you tell them?"

Holly swallowed before answering. "The number of his hotel room."

# Chapter 26

JONATHAN GROANED SOFTLY, and slowly opened his eyes, blinking at the bright light and the pounding in his skull. Blood trickled down the side of his face from where he'd been pistol-whipped.

He was seated in a chair with his hands tied behind him, strapping him to the weak wood. He fingered the knot, and his shoulders slumped slightly at the tightness of it. It wasn't coming undone easily.

At least he was still in his hotel room. That was something.

"Why are you stalling? Just do the job and let's go." The taller of his two captors pointed his gun at Jonathan as he said this. Neither of the men had noticed Jonathan was awake.

The heavyset shorter man shook his head. "This is bigger than that. We have him now. He is ours. Solak is not seeing the opportunity here."

"We have to follow orders. Solak says to kill, we kill. You shouldn't question him."

Jonathan's blood chilled. Yes, Hak Tanir had been trying to

kill him for the last month. They'd actually come close a few times, but this discussion instilled fear in him like he'd never known before.

"I'm tired of blindly following Solak's orders."

Jonathan closed his eyes, praying that the shorter man was the more dominant of the two. Whatever the man had planned for him wouldn't be good, but it beat being shot point-blank.

Jonathan opened his eyes in time to see both men's heads jerk toward the sound of his phone ringing.

*Abbie, where are you?*

# Chapter 27

"PICK UP, PICK UP, pick up." Abbie's words were an unheeded plea. Jonathan didn't answer her call, and the tiny knot of dread in the pit of her stomach snowballed into a wrecking ball that threatened to destroy her.

She whirled to face Holly. "If he dies, this is on you. All on you." Her voice was low and menacing. "You might as well have pulled the trigger yourself."

Holly's shoulders shook as she sobbed.

Abbie turned away from her, not wanting the cowardly woman in her line of sight. Then she proceeded to make the necessary calls—her security team and the local police. It nearly killed her to take the time, but she knew better than anyone that rushing into a hostage situation with guns blazing rarely turned out well. She needed to stay levelheaded for Jonathan's sake.

"Stay here," she ordered Holly, not bothering to wait for the woman's response before leaving the room. Holly would do as she was told, but the truth was Abbie didn't give a shit if

Holly tried to flee. She wouldn't be able to hide for long, and she just wasn't important right now.

In her room Abbie strapped on her weapons—shoulder piece, thigh piece, and a knife. She shrugged into her Kevlar vest on her way out the door.

*Stick to protocol. Follow procedure. This is just another job.*

Her heart wasn't hearing any of the bullshit she tried to feed it. It clenched and pounded in a way that made it hard to breathe.

*Pull it together, Whitmore. Jonathan needs you.*

She slipped in her earpiece. "Do we have eyes on the situation yet?"

"We're thirty seconds from the scene," came the response.

Goddamnit. What was taking so long? She glanced at her watch. It had been less than five minutes since she'd made the calls. Objectively speaking, that response time was excellent.

But personally speaking, it was way too long. Jonathan's life was at stake.

She quietly shut her door behind her and crept down the hall to Jonathan's room. She pressed her ear against the door, but the sounds were muffled.

Sounds were a good sign, though. People were inside. If they'd already...*completed the job,* they probably wouldn't have stuck around. Her stomach plummeted into her toes at the thought of her weak euphemism.

If only she had her surveillance equipment. This wasn't supposed to be a spying assignment, though—it was protection detail.

And that's exactly what she would do—protect Jonathan with her life.

She retrieved a glass from a room service tray that was sitting on the floor a few doors down and pressed it to the door. It was a primitive technique, but it allowed her to hear something that made the air *whoosh* out of her lungs in relief— Jonathan's voice.

There were two other voices as well. She didn't like those odds.

She crept back up the hall and put a hand to her earpiece. "Status?"

"There's a goddamn construction crane blocking the view from the next building. We're trying to resolve the issue. Stand by."

Goddamn construction crane was right. Even if they managed to get it moved, that might alert the perps. Construction cranes didn't just move in the middle of the night.

"Station SWAT outside the door. The perps are still unaware of our presence. I'm going in through the balcony."

She was breaking protocol. She should wait until backup was in place, but there was no way she could do that. Every minute Jonathan was alone with those assassins, he was another minute closer to dying.

## Chapter 28

LUCKILY, JONATHAN'S ROOM was on the third floor and not at the top of some high-rise hotel. Abbie looked down at the ground below and swallowed, her palms slick with sweat. Heights weren't really her thing. A three-story fall would hurt and might break a few bones.

The balconies were about six feet apart, so it shouldn't be difficult to scale the gap to Jonathan's balcony. As long as she didn't look down, anyway. But she went against her own advice and glanced at the ground below. Nausea washed over her.

She tried to remember if the blinds had been closed when she was there earlier for dinner. Of course, she hadn't noticed the crane sitting outside, so they'd probably been closed. She would've noticed that, right? Or was she losing her touch?

If they had been closed, that didn't mean they still were. He could have opened them. But why would he do that after midnight?

God, she was overanalyzing when she should be taking action. But the details had never seemed this important.

She threw one leg over the rail of the balcony, then the other. She said a silent prayer before leaping.

Her knees slammed into the rails of Jonathan's balcony with a loud clang. *Shit.* She hoped no one had heard that. Her toes touched down on the edge of his balcony ledge, and her fingers gripped the rails. She put one hand on her weapon and held her breath, waiting to see if anyone would come out to investigate the noise.

She counted to thirty and exhaled. Then she quickly scurried over the rail of the balcony.

She'd been half right about the blinds. They were partially open on the far side. With her back against the glass, she slid over and peeked through the opening.

She could barely see Jonathan. He was sitting in a chair facing away from her. His hands were tied behind his back, but she could tell by the rawness of the skin on his wrists and the frayed ends of the rope that he'd been working on the knots. It was remarkable he'd made any progress at all. Whoever had tied those knots knew what they were doing.

"Do not test me. I pledged loyalty to Solak."

"Solak or Hak Tanir? You have misguided loyalties, my friend."

Abbie flattened her back against the door as a tall, skinny man came into view.

"You have wasted too much time tonight. We need to finish the job before—"

"Don't talk to me about that anymore!"

A loud creak of metal sounded out in the distance, and Abbie looked over at the crane. Whatever idiot was in charge of moving it had chosen that moment to move the giant metal beast, and they had no idea what they were doing. It swayed dangerously close to the building.

Inside the room the two men started shouting.

*Shit.*

"Go now," Abbie said into her earpiece.

She fired her weapon at the top of the balcony door, shattering the glass, and raced through its frame just as the SWAT team flung open the other door. Four officers streaked in wearing tactical combat gear.

The shorter man immediately dropped his weapon and put his hands up, but the taller man spun around, frantically looking for a way out. Seeing that his options were blocked, he let out a cry.

"Long live Hak Tanir!" he screamed again, pointing his gun at Jonathan.

Abbie didn't think. She just reacted, diving into Jonathan and knocking his chair over, so that he crashed into the credenza.

The man fired two shots. One hit Abbie square in the chest. She felt the dull thud through the Kevlar. The other slammed into her shoulder near her collarbone.

She hit the ground hard.

A SWAT member overpowered the shooter, stripping him of his weapon and slamming him on the ground. He was still screaming about Hak Tanir as they cuffed him.

"Abbie! Abbie!"

It wasn't until she looked up to see Jonathan staring back at her that she felt the pain—a fire that burned in her shoulder. He was still tied to the chair, but other than an injury at his temple, he seemed to be fine.

*He's okay.*

She exhaled. The adrenaline left her body, and agony washed over her in torturous waves.

She reached out to put her hand on his cheek. "Don't worry. You're safe now."

Then she passed out.

# Chapter 29

JONATHAN RUSHED ALONGSIDE the gurney as the paramedics wheeled Abbie down the hotel hallway toward the elevator. She was still unconscious, despite all the IVs and shots they'd stuck in her.

There was so much blood. And she was so pale. It had taken the paramedics forever to get there. The SWAT team leader wouldn't let anyone in the room until they'd secured the perps and the premises.

They'd untied Jonathan immediately, and he'd applied pressure to Abbie's wound. He'd thought she was going to die on him right then and there. He didn't think shots near the collarbone were fatal, but what did he know? He knew blood loss was fatal, and she'd lost a lot of it.

She should have been protected by the Kevlar. It was a lucky shot on that bastard's part. As she'd leaped in front of Jonathan, her body had stretched at just the right angle for the bullet to hit home.

She'd taken a bullet for him.

It still hadn't fully sunk in. He was on autopilot, going through the motions.

*Goddamnit.* She needed to open her eyes.

They entered the elevator, went down to the main lobby and when the doors dinged, they wheeled her out to the parking lot. He grabbed hold of her hand and didn't let go.

As they crossed the pavement, he noticed Holly, handcuffed and sobbing, being put into the back of a police cruiser. *Unbelievable.* He would never have pegged her for the mole.

He felt a slight pressure as Abbie squeezed his hand. "That's right, baby. Open your eyes."

Her eyelids fluttered and then opened. It was obvious that it cost her to do so. She let out a little groan.

"I hear you, and I'm here for you." She panted and winced. "But don't ever call me baby."

The edges of his lips quirked up in a smile. "Did you just make a joke, Agent Whitmore? Now I know they're giving you the good drugs."

Abbie closed her eyes, but her mouth gave a small smile.

"We'll take good care of her, Congressman," the paramedic told him as she prepared to slide the gurney into the ambulance. Jonathan nodded, still reluctant to let go of Abbie's hand. He brought it to his lips before releasing it.

"Congressman, we should really take a look at your head."

Jonathan spared a glance at the remaining paramedic and nodded as he watched the ambulance whisk Abbie away with lights blazing and sirens blaring.

# Chapter 30

ABBIE LOWERED HERSELF back onto the bed, slapping away the hands of the matronly nurse.

The nurse frowned at her. "You should have called for assistance."

"My shoulder's hurt, not my legs." Sweat gathered on her forehead from the exertion it had taken her to make it to the bathroom and back. She probably should have called for a nurse, but she wasn't accustomed to asking for help every time she had to pee. If not for the agency's strict line-of-duty injury recovery policy, she would have checked herself out of the hospital already, even if it was against doctor's orders.

"I see you're being a model patient," Jonathan said drily. He leaned against the doorframe with a smirk on his face.

Abbie gave him a dirty look. "They're keeping me prisoner."

The nurse shook her head and clucked her tongue as she adjusted Abbie's bedding. Abbie gave her a dirty look, too.

"For you." From behind his back Jonathan pulled a bouquet of pink, red, and yellow roses mixed with white and purple lilies. He stepped into the room as the nurse left, closing the door behind her.

"Thanks," Abbie said. "You can put them next to the standard-issue flower arrangement from the agency." Every injured agent received the same gift—twenty stems of mums of various colors. She would know. When she first started at the agency years ago, it had been her job to order them. She'd almost laughed when they'd arrived.

Jonathan placed the flowers on the table. "It's the Smiles and Sunshine bouquet, so naturally, it made me think of you."

"Sorry." Abbie grimaced. She was being a total bitch. "They're lovely. Really. I just don't like hospitals. They don't bring out the best in me."

"So I've noticed," Jonathan commented. He sat on the edge of her bed. "I visited Holly."

Abbie's eyebrows shot up. He was a better person than she was.

"She was very apologetic," Jonathan continued. "And she's doing everything she can to cooperate with police. Her sister has been located. They're working to extract her now."

"That's good. I still can't believe Holly didn't turn to you first. She had to have known you'd help her."

"Fear makes people do stupid things." He laced her fingers in his, rubbing his thumb over the top of her hand. His touch made her heart beat faster but was soothing at the same time.

"I guess you've heard by now that the one prisoner is spilling everything he knows about Hak Tanir?"

"Yes, that's contributed to how they managed to find Hannah so quickly."

Abbie nodded. The agency had been keeping her in the loop, but she was not as informed as she would be if she were on the inside. All the more reason to break out of these institutionalized white walls.

"How are you feeling?" Concern shone in his eyes.

Abbie shrugged. "I've been better. But overall, not bad."

"I still can't believe you took a bullet for me."

"It's my job."

"You're very good at it." He paused. "Can I kiss you?"

She looked at him with a bewildered expression. "Why are you even asking that? I was shot, but I'm not broken."

She leaned forward and grabbed hold of his shirt, then pulled him closer until her mouth crushed into his. He reached up and cupped her face, deepening the kiss. His lips were greedy, his tongue demanding yet tender. She met his urgency with her own. Heat began to build within her. She ran her hand over the hard muscles of his chest.

After a moment he pulled away and rested his forehead against hers. "How much longer until the doctor clears you?"

She leaned back on the bed, her shoulder aching dully. "Too long."

Jonathan's eyes met hers, and in them she found a need that

matched her own. He pulled his gaze away and stood, going to the door to retrieve a gift bag he'd left there.

"This is your real gift. The flowers were just a teaser."

He placed the bag on the edge of the bed. She reached in, pulling out a plain tan shoe box with white lettering that she knew well.

She squealed and hugged the box to her chest for a moment before tearing open the lid. Inside were the most perfect pair of red-soled stilettos she'd ever seen. No grass stains. No dangling heel. No wine splatters. She ran her finger along the smooth black leather. *Perfect.*

"I would like to say 'you shouldn't have,' but we both know I'd be lying." She grinned. "Thank you, Jonathan. I love them."

"I figured I owed you a pair." His expression turned serious. "Listen, when we get back to Washington, I'd like our relationship to be official. Public."

She swallowed, not sure how to answer. She had grown to like him—and care for him deeply—but was she really in a place where she could have a relationship? She couldn't answer that question, but she did know she'd regret letting him walk out of her life. Hell, she made a living by skating through dangerous situations. She could handle another one in her personal life, right? Because she was dangerously close to falling head over gorgeous red-soled heels for him.

She took a deep breath. "I can't promise anything—"

He put his hands up. "I get that. Neither can I. Our schedules—"

"Are crazy." They looked at each other in silence for a moment before Abbie spoke again. "I'd like that. I'd like to see where this goes."

The self-assured politician's smile that she'd grown to love graced his face, then he lowered his lips to hers.

She melted into his kiss, for once feeling okay with not being in control.

## About the Author

JESSICA LINDEN lives in Virginia with her college-sweetheart husband, two rambunctious sons, and two rowdy but lovable rescue dogs. Since her house is overflowing with testosterone, it's a good thing she has a healthy appreciation for Marvel movies, Nerf guns, and football.

# HE'S WORTH MILLIONS, BUT HE'S WORTHLESS WITHOUT HER.

After a traumatic breakup with her billionaire boyfriend, Derick, Siobhan Dempsey moves to Detroit, where she can build her painting career on her own terms. But Derick wants her back. And though Siobhan's body comes alive at his touch, she doesn't know if she can trust him again....

# READ THE STEAMY SECOND BOOK IN THE DIAMOND TRILOGY, *RADIANT,* COMING SOON FROM

**THE BEAR MOUNTAIN DAYS ARE COLD, BUT THE NIGHTS ARE STEAMY....**

Allie Fairchild made a mistake when she moved to Montana. Her rental is a mess, her coworkers at the trauma center are hostile, and her handsome landlord, Dex Belmont, is far from charming. But just when she's about to throw in the towel, life in Bear Mountain takes a surprisingly sexy turn....

# HOT WINTER NIGHTS
# BY
# CODI GARY

**READ THE SCORCHING ROMANCE,**
***HOT WINTER NIGHTS*, COMING SOON FROM**

# THE GOLDEN BOY OF FOOTBALL JUST WENT *BAD*.

Quarterback Grayson Knight has a squeaky-clean reputation—except when he's suddenly arrested for drug possession. Even though she's on the opposing side of the courtroom, DA's assistant Melissa St. James wants desperately to help him—and he desperately wants her....

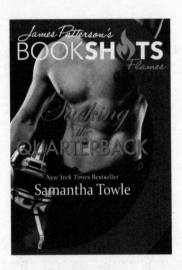

**Read about their thrilling affair in *Sacking the Quarterback,* available now from**

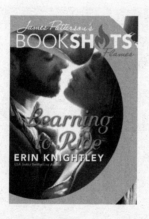

## "I'M NOT ON TRIAL. SAN FRANCISCO IS."

Drug cartel boss the Kingfisher has a reputation for being violent and merciless. And after he's finally caught, he's set to stand trial for his vicious crimes—until he begins unleashing chaos and terror upon the lawyers, jurors, and police associated with the case. The city is paralyzed, and Detective Lindsay Boxer is caught in the eye of the storm.

Will the Women's Murder Club make it out alive—or will a sudden courtroom snare ensure their last breaths?

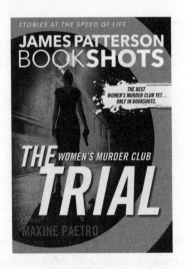

**Read the shocking new Women's Murder Club story, available now only from**

# BOOK**SHOTS**

## "ALEX CROSS, I'M COMING FOR YOU...."

Gary Soneji, the killer from *Along Came a Spider,* has been
dead for more than ten years—but Cross swears he saw
Soneji gun down his partner. Is Cross's worst enemy back
from the grave?

Nothing will prepare you for the wicked truth.

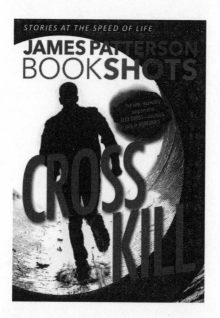

**Read the next riveting, pulse-racing Alex Cross
adventure, available now only from**

# BOOK**SHOTS**